GUILT RIDDEN

THE WALKER FIVE, BOOK 4

MARIE JOHNSTON

LE PUBLISHING

The one that got away…

Travis Walker thought he'd gotten over his high school crush when she moved away to get married. But Kami's widowed and back in town with her daughter—and the timing couldn't be worse. He's thrown himself into work since his fiancée's sudden death. And he happens to be interested in expanding his own operation by purchasing the land Kami's mom is selling.

Kami Preston has failed at everything else in life, but she's desperate to keep her mom's land in the family. The dream of opening her own gymnastics studio will have to collect dust like all the old junk her dad had shoved in the barn. Suddenly she's in over her head, trying to figure out how to run a farm and ranch.

Travis should be rooting for her to fail, but he's there to help every step of the way, and Kami needs every ounce of help he offers. The more they're together, the easier it is to wonder what might have been…and now just might be her chance to find out.

For all the latest news, sneak peeks, quarterly short stories, and free material sign up for my newsletter.

It's always hard for me to write a catty mother-in-law because mine is a rockstar. To my MIL.

—————

For new release updates and chapter sneak peeks, sign up for Marie's newsletter via instaFreebie and receive a FREE novella from my Fleet Romance series.

CHAPTER 1

*H*eavy drops of rain splattered the windshield. Dark blue clouds unleashed their watery load until Travis had to flip his wipers to high just to keep up. The sound of a downpour filled the cab of his Ford F150. He could turn the radio up to help drown it out but was reluctant to take his hands off the wheel. Easing up on the accelerator, he slowed to sixty, far under the interstate speed limit.

Headlights approached from behind. A semi veered into the passing lane and plowed past, spraying a tidal wave of surface water in its wake.

"Asshole." Travis punched the defogger and twisted the volume to the radio while he was at it. A country song full of metaphors about sex and driving smothered the rainfall's noise. It sounded way more upbeat than a tense night of driving in the middle of a storm.

Why the hell had he decided to head to Fargo tonight?

Because what he had to do couldn't wait.

Michelle's warm brown eyes flashed in his mind. Her eyes were what had attracted him when he'd passed her on campus that first time. Then they'd had a lab together and eventually, he'd gotten her talking to him.

But lately, those intelligent eyes hadn't been as happy, not as bright and full of life. Tonight, he was going to do something about it. They'd broken up twice already in their four-year relationship, and while they were back together, Travis felt like they were hanging in a limbo. She stayed in Fargo, not yet willing to uproot herself to live with him in Moore, Minnesota.

I can't move my life just because we're in a relationship.

She wanted a commitment. He had two of the three things he wanted in life—his home and his farm. But the two he had weren't compatible with the third—his woman.

Travis pinched the bridge of his nose. Yeah, it was time. Unfortunately, he'd made his decision during the first thunderstorm of the spring season. But once his mind was made up, he wasn't the type to sit on it.

The rain eased until it was a steady fall and not a torrent. Billboards flashed by. Fifteen more miles.

At the first exit with a sizable truck stop, he pulled off. He couldn't just go to Michelle's empty-handed, not that anything would really go with what he had to talk to her about.

He browsed past the rack of droopy flowers and over-priced knick-knacks, choosing instead an iced tea and a bag of Hershey's kisses, Michelle's favorite. He reached the counter and stared at the treats in his hands. Spinning on a heel, he stuffed each one back where he'd gotten it. For a night like this, nothing would be adequate.

He was back on the road in minutes. With the rain, he stayed off the interstate and wove through town to the north side. Her condo was by campus, where she worked as an adjunct professor in the food science department.

The roads glistened under the streetlights. He finally

allowed himself to relax, just a little. He shrugged to loosen his shoulders and rolled his neck.

It was going to be okay. He and Michelle had their whole life in front of them.

He frowned when he reached her street. More cars than normal blocked the front. A shot of panic zinged down his spine. She didn't have company, did she?

He drove past her place to turn around and park on the other side of the street. Her living room light glowed in the dark, but he couldn't tell if anyone else was there.

He sauntered across the road, hands shoved into his jeans pocket to ward off the chill. He didn't rush, but took the extra time while rain splattered his face to run through what he'd say.

The blue front door loomed in front of him. He clamped his teeth together and dug Michelle's extra key out of his pocket. They'd had each other's key for years, but never shared a roof. Letting himself in, he shivered involuntarily.

Scowling at the landing of her split foyer, a sense of dread washed over him. Were those voices?

They had a tinny quality. Must be TV.

He toed off his Ariats and set them aside. Should he call for her? His only worry was that he'd scare the shit out of her, and that wasn't how he wanted to start the night.

Brushing his damp hair off his forehead, he went upstairs where the sole light was on. The voices grew louder.

Yep, her TV was on, and the grim voice of the narrator described a husband's mournful last words about his deceased wife. How odd. She never watched true crimes shows, claimed they scared her too much before bed. She usually settled on HGTV in the evening. Nothing like a little Property Brothers to inspire her dreams.

Her favorite recliner faced the TV, her hand draped over the side.

"Hey, Michelle. Did you hear me come in?"

Nothing but the TV answered him. It was evening, not late enough for her to fall asleep in the chair, a habit she didn't normally have. But that'd explain her choice of television if she hadn't been awake to change the channel.

"Michelle?" He crossed to her. Damn, had she fallen asleep? What he had to do couldn't be done with a groggy Michelle. "Hey, Michelle. Wake up, sleepy head."

She didn't move. Her head slumped to her chest and her body slanted off kilter. A sense of wrongness descended.

"Michelle!" Dropping to his knees, he grabbed her hand. When his fingers touched her cool skin, his heart plummeted.

He croaked her name again, barely recognizing his own voice. He tugged on her hand, but it was no use.

She was gone.

For a moment, his mind blanked. Then a rush of questions clogged his thinking. Should he try CPR? Should he call her parents? Call the police? What if she wasn't really dead?

Releasing a long breath, he allowed his gaze to sweep over her. Lifeless. Pale. He placed her limp hand on the armrest, unwilling to let it hang uselessly. With his hand on hers, he stared at the connection, his mind sluggish.

Then he dug out his phone and dialed 9-1-1.

TRAVIS SAT on the front steps, his hands propped on his knees. His fingers were so cold, they were on the painful side of numb. A few more minutes and the pain would cede to complete numbness. Lingering rain seeped through his pants, and the only light cast was from the lone streetlight on Michelle's side of the street.

Michelle's parents were inside the condo. They had

nowhere else to stay and suddenly found themselves with a daughter to bury and a funeral to plan. He didn't know how they were going to do it. He'd stick around until Michelle's brother arrived from the East Coast.

The door opened behind him, but he didn't care who it was.

"Come on inside, Travis," Michelle's dad, Phil, said. "Sitting out here in the cold won't bring her back."

The man's voice cracked. Travis imagined him trying to hold his tears back. Why bother? No one was going to call them out for the shock and grief they felt over suddenly losing a child. Michelle might've been twenty-seven, but she'd always be their baby.

Travis of all people knew how close she'd been with her parents.

Scrubbing his face with frigid fingers, he sighed. Yeah, he'd better head inside. He stood, and when he turned, more figurative weight piled on his shoulders. The man looked like he'd aged a decade or more within four hours.

"Della's lying down in the guest room." Phil shut and locked the door after Travis stepped into the warm but no longer inviting foyer. "I don't know where you'll..." His throat worked, but he couldn't say the words.

Right. Would he sleep in the bed he and Michelle had made love in too many times to count? Or would he sleep on the couch, next to the recliner she took her last breath in? He'd have to take that chair back to the farm and burn it. None of them could ever sit in it, but they couldn't give it away, not with what they'd lost in it.

"I'll find a spot to rest. Don't worry about me." God, the last thing he wanted was for them to waste any concern on him.

Phil nodded and dropped his gaze. "I appreciate you staying here to help us. I was... I'm, um, really sorry. You were always a part of the family." His eyes welled with tears, and he choked on a sob. "And now you'll never be."

The man nearly collapsed. Travis's throat burned, but he had yet to shed a tear. He pulled Phil in for a hug, afraid the man would drop on the laminate floor without the support.

As Phil shook with sobs, Travis stared at the wall. He hadn't shed any tears yet, but it was a matter of time. He'd do it when it wouldn't burden Michelle's parents. And after witnessing how hard the shock impacted them, Travis made one private resolution.

No one, *no one*, was ever going to know he'd come here to break off his engagement.

CHAPTER 2

ifteen months later...

Kami Preston nailed the eight ball into the corner pocket and grinned. "What do I get when I win again, Austin?"

Her on-again, off-again—mostly off—ex scowled at the pool table. "You've been practicing, Preston." He racked his pool stick. "But what else are you going to do, am I right?"

She bristled at his dig but hid it with a swig of beer. "You mean between my two jobs?" Three if she counted being a parent, but she didn't. She mentally snorted. Austin probably would, but her ten-year-old angel, Kambria, only turned into a little devil around him.

And that's why she only saw Austin when Kambria was with her grandparents. If she wanted to be a little shit with them, Kami wouldn't punish her. Why her daughter got so defensive with Austin but didn't bat an eye when Kami's former in-laws threw shade on her, she'd never know. Might as well take the support where she could get it.

Sliding onto her stool, she eyed Austin. Why did her

daughter dislike him so much? He had a job, dressed respectably, didn't swear around her. Kami and Austin had dated in high school, but depending on who you asked, many would say she "dated" everyone in high school.

They'd be right. But that was high school, and she was determined not to be that girl again. So she stuck with Austin when she needed adult company.

Austin crowded behind her, his hands on her biceps as he bent to nibble her neck.

"Dude, we're in public." She scanned the rest of the bar. No one paid them any attention. Anyone who was a halfway regular here was used to seeing the two of them playing pool and hanging out.

At least she'd get to have a beer and a break from serving others all day, instead of just having sex and going home alone. Austin didn't seem to mind as long as he knew where they'd end up.

At least nasty rumors wouldn't worm their way to her daughter about her if she stuck to hooking up with just one guy. All the other good ones in Moore were taken or thought she was as disposable as she'd been in high school.

No. That wasn't true. One of the good ones was dead.

She cleared her suddenly thick throat. God, memories of Ben haunted her at the most inopportune times.

To change the subject, she pulled a piece of paper out of her pocket. "Take a look at this."

Austin gave up his amorous efforts and moved a stool next to her. He snapped the sheet out of her fingers and peered at it. His handsome features morphed with doubt and he raised a dark brow at her.

"What?" she asked. *Don't you dare be an asshole about this!*

"Why are you walking around with an ad for an old grocery store in your pocket?"

The jury was still out on how he was going to react. "Look at the price."

"And?" The attitude he threw into the word raised her defenses.

"I want to buy it and convert it into a gymnastics academy." Forcing herself to sound firm and confident, she clenched her hands together to aid her in the effort. She was going out on a limb telling him, but if anyone knew what it meant to her, he would. "You did know the one in Moore shut down years ago, right? It'd be good for the community to have one again."

He raised both brows, his expression screaming, *You're shitting me?*

"I think I can swing it. I've kept current by coaching part-time in Normandy." Her confidence wavered. *No, Kami!* She'd thought this through, and yes, she was lacking credentials, but where there was a will, there was a way. Where there was desperation not to work herself into the ground doing a job that could just as well pay in beans, there was a way. And she'd find it.

Austin flicked the paper back to her and reclined with his beer. "You need to do more than think, Kami. Fuck, just because you coached in high school doesn't make you qualified to manage a freaking business. Most of those things are alive because of sponsors and fund-raisers and that's a whole 'nother beast."

She rescued the advertisement and nestled it back in her pocket. Why'd she show him, again? "I know that 'beast.' I helped the old director do all of that."

He scoffed and took a swig of his beer. "Sorry to tell ya, it's more than wearing a tight leotard and washing cars in the gas station parking lot."

She ground her teeth before telling him to shove it until he choked on his drink.

If you aren't going to ride at the top, quit humiliating yourself. Her dad's words echoed through her head as brutally as when he'd been alive.

"Come on, Preston." Austin shot her the humoring expression he used to give her daughter before Kambria asked him if he was constipated. "Being a business owner is hard enough, but it's…you."

Why'd she think telling him was a good idea? Was nostalgia a strong enough reason? They'd always come back together as teens, he'd been what she knew before she threw all she knew away and got married.

Keeping her tone even, she asked, "What do you mean by that?"

"You ran off and got married when you got knocked up. Did you ever take a college class? Even step on a campus?" He lowered his voice in an attempt to make her understand his complete lack of faith in her. "Remember our panicked study sessions? We both barely graduated, and you at the end of senior year, all up in your morning sickness. Stick to what you know. Raise your kid. But don't throw your money away."

Stick to what you know. So much like what her dad would say. Was that why she gravitated back to Austin since she'd moved home? Uprooting herself after graduation to get married and have the baby that was already on its way hadn't been an attempt at preventing single motherhood.

It had been because Ben was so different from anyone else. Well, except for—

No, she wouldn't think about him. Ben had been like her. Normal. Mediocre, but in all the good ways. She'd ran off, confident no one would've looked at Ben and said, "What's he doing with *her?*"

Austin chuckled and shook his head. "That must've been

some life insurance. Why don't you just buy a decent place for you and the kid. At least you'd have that going for you."

The kid.

Stick to what you know.

At least you'd have that going for you.

It was time to be done being with a guy that made her feel stupid. Inadequate.

She dug in her purse and withdrew a ten-dollar bill. Tossing it on the table, she met his confused gaze. "I think we're done here. Go ahead and delete my number from your contacts."

"Kam—"

She held up her hand as she walked away. "I'll be busy with my *kid.*"

"Seriously?" he called, but he didn't come after her. That was because it'd require work on his part, and she'd made it too easy for him.

The spot between her shoulder blades twitched. The other customers in the bar were watching her leave, probably wondering why she wasn't leaving with Austin. Likely assumed she'd be here with him the next time her kid was on an overnighter.

Normally, they'd be right.

Kami growled at the weak-willed stupidity she'd slipped back into. But, dammit, being with Austin was better than sitting alone in her house, thinking of how proud Ben would be of his daughter.

She plowed out the door and right into a fabric-covered wall.

"Whoa."

Strong hands steadied her as she stared at an expanse of green that accentuated a nicely muscular chest. Her gaze drifted up, and heat crept into her face.

Because this night wasn't humiliating enough.

"Sorry, Travis." She stepped back and brushed her hair off her face. Usually it was thrown back in a ponytail, but she tried to give at least half an effort when she had a sort-of date night. Right now, she was glad she had. She never crossed this close to the brains in the Walker Five farm and ranch operation, Travis Walker.

Well, once she had. It felt like forever ago, and God, she hoped he didn't remember.

Look at her being foolish again. A man remembered who took his virginity.

"You okay?" His grin faded, replaced with concern. "You banged out the door like it was your worst enemy."

Her veins still ran hot with Austin's immediate dismissal of her dream, but she attempted to sound light. "The door took the brunt for someone else."

Her breathing was calming down. Standing next to Travis eased the tangle of her emotions, and in an instant, she was transported to ten years ago when she flirted with a gawkier Travis Walker. To her surprise, he'd taken her up on her offer to hang out…on a weekend night…alone…

And he'd rocked her world in the backseat of his pickup with only a million stars as witness.

How a virgin had known to do what he'd done…

But, word got out in a small town. A few of her fellow cheerleaders had seen them driving around together and the catty comments started.

Do you really think Travis is interested in you for more than a hookup? I mean, he's a hot nerd, but still a nerd.

"Kami?"

He was talking to her. She pressed her fingers against her temples and played it off as irritation with Austin. "Sorry, I missed what you said. I was supposed to be on a date, but…"

His brilliant blue eyes twinkled. "But Austin is acting like himself?"

Her mouth dropped open. She snapped it shut, but her lips twitched. "He was definitely being Austin. So, what are you doing here? I haven't seen you around in forever." A slow burn of sorrow washed over her as she remembered. "I'm really sorry about your fiancée."

His smile was sincere, but sadness swam in his gaze. "Thanks. My cousins coaxed me to come out, but I'm not feeling really sociable. It was never really my scene anyway." Again, he soothed her embarrassment with a smile. "But I am really hungry. This place has atrocious pizza, and I don't see any of their trucks in the lot, yet. Care to head to—"

"Anywhere but Tyler's Club." She meant it as a joke. Her second job was bartending at a local bar, but she realized too late that it sounded like she accepted his offer.

"Great. The Brown House Cafe doesn't have pizza, but their omelets are killer."

Should she correct him, tell him she'd been joking? Make an excuse that she had to get home? Austin was behind her in the bar, and her tiny apartment was down the street. Spending an hour with Travis was hands down better than either option.

How long had it been since his fiancée died? It wasn't long before she'd moved back a year ago. No matter how long had passed, she knew how sitting by oneself after a loss was sometimes the hardest thing to do.

"As long as I get your hash browns."

He grinned and her belly clenched. The man got more potent with age.

Think of all the bedroom tricks he'd learned since then.

Immediately, guilt flooded back. He'd just said he wasn't feeling sociable. He was only being nice, felt sorry for her because everyone knew Austin…and Travis would know she couldn't do better.

He dug keys out of his pocket. "Wanna hop in with me? I'll text the guys that I decided not to come."

"Sure. I live close enough that I walked here." She could even walk to the cafe, it was only a little over a mile, but it was night, and he offered.

She strolled with him, chatting about the calm June night with little wind. He opened the passenger door to his blue Ford pickup.

Studying the inside, she developed a major case of vehicle envy. During her family's best days farming, they could never afford a ride like this. If Ben hadn't left behind a sensible car, she'd be pouring her scant money into the same pickup she drove in high school, sitting by the barn at her mom's.

He fired up the engine and pulled out of the lot. "When'd you move back to Moore?"

Since everyone knew her story, she let it spill. "We came home about a year ago, thought I'd help Mom and she'd help me." And to get away from Ben's parents. Their meddling had been an annoyance when Ben was alive. After his death, they dabbled in being controlling, manipulative. So she'd used the excuse that she'd move home and help her mom. Lord knew, Mom needed it.

But there was a part of her that wanted to give Kambria more in life, and she could do that with Mom's place. Land for Kambria to run, semi-tame cats for her to wrangle, and someday, if Kami planned right, a horse.

"How old is your daughter?"

Kami couldn't keep the smile out of her voice. "Kambria's ten. You know, ten going on twenty-five. So much attitude, it's ridiculous. And she hated me for moving here, but she survived her first year in a new school."

"And where are you working?"

She wanted to sigh. A guy that ran a successful business in a tough industry wasn't going to be impressed by her lack of a resume.

"I bartend at Tyler's Club and wait tables at Old Main." She cringed, waiting for the smartest man she'd ever met to comment on her career trajectory like every other adult in her life.

"Two jobs? Must keep you busy."

Letting out the breath she'd been holding, she studied his handsome profile. Strong nose, square jawline, a touch of lankiness that gave him the farm boy appeal and not the former football star appeal like Austin. She remembered Travis had played football, but he'd been there in body only, never as enthusiastic as the other players. Even going through the motions, he'd been a decent player, but he had been much more engaged in class. And in the backseat.

Being in the same vehicle with him transported her back over eleven years.

He parked, and she hopped out. They strode into the sparse cafe. Only one server was working, and thankfully it was a young girl Kami didn't recognize. She didn't need gossip spread through town that she'd moved on to yet another man.

When she'd hooked up with Austin after she moved home, word spread like a prairie fire and her mom had called her. *They're saying you barely covered Ben with dirt before you were in Austin's bed.*

She clenched her jaw and fought to keep tears from welling. Whether people in town really had noticed, or Mom lied to keep Kami from dating, it hurt.

As she slid into the booth, she couldn't help but think they'd still say that about her, but not about Travis, who'd also lost someone recently, too. Yet here he was.

~

Travis didn't want to take his eyes off Kami as she read the menu. He'd seen her in passing since she'd moved back, knew the wild, vivacious girl he'd known had turned into a calmer version as a woman. But he worried she had lost her spark.

In high school, she held nothing back. Loudest to cheer, first to party, she'd been known to bust out a cartwheel mid-conversation. Tonight, she was reserved, almost hesitant.

Was she like him and just wanted to go home? He had a new issue of *Progressive Farmer* waiting for him. He'd almost procrastinated on leaving his house to read the article on the new Enlist E3 soybean. Good thing he hadn't, or he would've missed Kami.

His family kept pestering him to get out. The few times he had, they went to the usual places. The same crowd would be out and nothing had changed. Just because he was single now didn't make it any more appealing. He'd rather be working on his second Farmland game, since a lot of his spare swaths of time was spent helping Michelle's parents. Losing their daughter had devastated them, and leaning on Travis for help around their own farm was how they coped.

Then he'd come home, where everyone felt bad for him. And yeah, he missed Michelle. But the looks and whispers were about a man who wouldn't get to marry the woman of his dreams, a man who lost his future.

He'd lost a friend. A really good friend. He and Michelle would've always been on good terms. Maybe they would've crossed paths in the agriculture industry, chatted and caught up on life, then parted ways to their separate paths.

But no one knew that. They thought it was a great tragedy for him. He hated the attention, as if he didn't feel guilty enough. Michelle's parents said they felt like they lost him, too. Their words tore him up inside, so he helped them out more. They had enough to worry about, needed to take care of themselves, not be concerned with how he was doing. He hated that they spent one ounce of worry on him.

But all his inner turmoil faded when he looked at Kami.

Like a spring breeze, she'd charged out of that bar and into him, saving him from another pathetic night.

What the hell did she see in Austin? Hopefully, she'd quit seeing him.

She glanced at him, a question in her eyes.

And he was leering at her like the dork he'd been in school. "Sorry, what?"

"What kind of omelet are you getting?"

"There's only one kind—the Everything Omelet."

She smiled and closed her menu, her rich brown eyes full of humor. "Then I'll have what you're having."

"All right, but get your own hash browns. I don't share."

He shoved the menus to the edge and reclined. If he could go back and tell his seventeen-year-old self that he might have another chance with Kami Lee English, he'd do it in a heartbeat. The crush he'd fostered for years had been blown to bits after their earth-shattering night together when she'd hooked back up with Austin the next weekend.

Oh, Travis had heard the gossip in high school. All his friends had told him he was too good for her. A wild child raised by a single mom who had earned her own reputation before she'd settled down with Kami's grouch of a dad.

Kami was—had been—carefree. But they'd rode the bus together all through elementary school and middle school. He knew her. She had a good heart and gave it away too easily. It was probably for the best she'd left him in the glow of the taillights. It was more like she left him sitting in an empty parking lot for hours after their agreed upon meet time. He would've been wrapped around her finger so hard, he wouldn't have left her side.

Instead, he'd gone to college. Gone to more college. Met Michelle and…

He took a sip of water. Again, the thought of Michelle brought the dull ache of sadness and a whole heap of guilt. Despite her breaking up with him twice to entice him to leave the farm and move to Fargo, he couldn't get over what his goal had been as she'd taken her last breath.

"How are you doing, Travis?" Kami's soft voice shattered his thoughts.

His expression must have broadcasted what was going on in his mind. "I'm fine."

She tapped the back of his hand and shot him a knowing look. "How are you *really* doing?"

He should've realized he wouldn't be able to bullshit her. She'd lost a husband, and while he'd had the intention to break up with Michelle, he'd still lost a fiancée.

"I miss her, but I feel worse for her family. I mean, her parents were…destroyed, obviously."

"They will be for a long time."

He considered her frank statement. She seemed so much more at ease with this subject, and she'd actually been married and had a kid. How'd she move on?

For one, she'd moved back home. Did her in-laws cling to her for support?

"Can I ask you something?"

She nodded, and he continued.

"How was it living in the same town after he died? How'd you do it, moving back *here*? Michelle wasn't from Moore, either, but enough people knew her, and if they didn't, they at least knew I was engaged. I can't go anywhere without—" He clapped his mouth shut when the young server appeared at their table.

They ordered, and the server moved on, but Travis didn't finish what he'd been saying. Saying it made him feel like too much of an ass, like he was ungrateful people actually cared.

"You can't go anywhere without the looks."

So he wasn't crazy. "God, yes."

"And the reassuring comments."

"I don't want to dread them, but I do."

She nodded. "In a way, they were comforting. I hung on to the thought that he was in a better place, took reassurance from it. But another part of me grew to hate some of the statements. They made me think, gee, thanks for assuming life with me was hell. Ben was in a car accident. It's not like he was sick for months or years, not like he'd been suffering. We had a good life." A sad smile lifted her lips. "Simple, but good."

"Is that why you came back?"

She shook her head, and under the dim cafe lights, her hair glowed as gold as a ripe wheat field. "The people in town were amazing. I had a lot of emotional support—when I needed it and when I didn't want it. Mostly when I didn't want it," she muttered. "But I couldn't move on with my life there. Mom's here, and shift work as a single mom is the worst juggling act."

Had over ten years really passed since she'd gotten married? Their senior year, Kami had gotten pregnant by a football player in Normandy, an hour away. Not long after their graduation ceremony, he heard she'd up and moved to be with the dad.

He and Kami had taken much different routes after school, but they were both here. And she'd mentioned her mom.

"How's your mom doing?"

Kami's expression turned guarded. "What happened? Did she yell at you about something?"

He chuckled. They weren't exactly feuding families. Their land bordered each other's, and Kami's dad and his dad had butted heads more than once. If one of his family's cattle got out, Earl English raised hell and demanded reimbursement for every blade of grass the cow ate. If one of their tractors so much as grazed an inch of his land, he was pointing out the damage before they shut the engine off.

Earl had passed away years ago. Travis and his cousins wouldn't mind if Kami's mom, Pam, came charging out. It might mean she gave a shit about any of her acreage.

But they'd heard rumors… Pam English was considering selling. And his family was considering expanding.

"I heard she was thinking of putting her place up for sale." The house would have to be demolished, or burned. Useless. They could expand their herd up to four hundred head, two hundred cattle in each pasture. Then they could grow silage for their stock in the neighboring field.

Kami's face lost all expression. "What do you mean?"

"Maybe it was just farmer gossip, but she's seeing Doc Granger, and he told Dale at the parts store, who mentioned something to Brock." Why'd Kami look so stunned? It should've been good news, a lot less stressful life for her mom. Weird that Pam hadn't told her, but maybe Doc was full of shit. "Anyway, it's perfect for expanding our ranching operation. Think you could put in a good word?"

"Dad would roll over in his grave if the Walkers got his land." Kami shook her head and her gaze darted around the restaurant. She didn't seem to notice the server delivering their food.

"I understand. Our parents had their issues, but it's not being cared for. It'd make sense for her to sell."

Her brow furrowed. "She'd never sell to you."

He stared at her for a moment, couldn't understand her reaction. Her expression was offended, but her body language defensive. "Honestly, though. Who would buy it? Even if she sold at a reasonable price, it's still three quarters of land, the eight acres the house is on, and the back forty your dad used to keep the horses in. Unless she piecemealed it out, who's going to afford to buy it? I guess she can always rent it out." He shook his head. "I have no clue why she hadn't been doing that since your dad passed."

Kami's expression darkened, her jaw tightened. Was this discussion making her angry? That was the last effect he wanted on Kami Lee English—Preston. How could he forget? Kami Lee Preston.

He strove to explain his reasoning. "See, even if others could afford the price tag, they'd still need people to work it. But in order to afford it, they're already working pretty hard, right? It's not common someone's going to suddenly take up ranching, so if your mom lists it, then she might sit on it for months. Years."

He stopped talking, hoping she'd agree wholeheartedly. There was no ill will between him and her mom. The Walker Five snatching up that property would be the best thing for Pam.

Kami worked her jaw, her gaze slanted on him. He waited for her to talk, afraid he'd dig himself into a larger hole and still not know why.

She touched one of her pockets, her gaze introspective. With a look of resolve, she sat up straighter and ran her tongue across her teeth. Her shoulders were wide and her chin high. This was the Kami he remembered. The girl who dominated Powder Puff football night their senior year because the other team had said that third grade boys could run faster and tackle harder than them. Powder Puff used flags, but Kami had gotten some tackles in that night.

"Say my mom is selling. I may have the money."

It was his turn to wear the shocked look. He managed to

keep his jaw closed. Could Kami make an offer? How could she have that much cash available? To finance, she'd need a sizeable down payment. Then there was the old double-wide manufactured home that needed too much work. It was better to build new.

Not that he'd move there. He had his home, the one he'd literally been born in, thanks to a winter due date and drifted-in roads, and he'd raise his own family there one day.

He and his cousins had talked about how they'd leave the lot empty and if his brother or sister or one of his other cousins ever moved home, they could build. Otherwise, they'd have to hire additional help in order to expand.

But that was him and four cousins he worked with. Who'd Kami have?

"Is it just you?"

She kicked her chin out. "Yes. Me and Kambria."

He pushed his plate to the side and folded his hands on the table. The steam from the omelets was dwindling; neither of them had touched their food. If he could only get her to see that she'd be better off using her money with some other venture. "It's going to be excessively difficult to do on your own. You'll have the cost of buying the place, but then there's buying stock. Although you'd probably qualify for a low-interest loan for new farmers. Leafy spurge has filled the pastures, and while it's not impossible to get cows to graze in it, it can take time and patience. Did you know that your mom sold all the equipment after she sold off her cattle? Hauling bales to the herd is going to be impossible without a tractor."

Kami leaned over the table. "You're so certain I can't do it."

The venom of her tone caught him off guard.

It must be hard for her to give up the place she'd grown up in. But the land itself would need a lot of cleaning before they could plant any cover crops for feed. The pastures were full of junk—the top half of an old bus that was used for a calving shelter, twisted fencing wire, and the old cars... His dad had suspected Kami's mom accepted money from people who wanted to dump vehicles and old tractors. Easy money for little to no work. The effect was a blemish on the land. Ugly, twisted metal marred the natural beauty of the pastures.

"Kami, that place needs a lot of work before it can make any kind of money."

"And you think I don't know that?" Her voice raised in both volume and pitch. And while her anger only intensified her strength and beauty, he didn't want it directed at him.

Holding his hands up, he tried to diffuse the explosive potential of the conversation. "I didn't say anything about your capabilities. But..."

It was the "but" that ruined his attempt. He knew it as soon as it left his mouth.

"But what? But I'm a single mom? But I have no college degree? But the only thing I'm good at is pouring drinks and picking up men? Take your pick of all the buts I've been told my whole life. Here's a but for you—" she smacked the table with the flat of her hand and the ice in their glasses clinked, "—I have the money and I'm buying my home."

She slid out of the booth.

"Wait!"

She spun around, fire blazing in her gaze.

He frantically searched for a way to keep her from leaving. The cooling food on the table was the best reason he could come up with. "You didn't touch your plate."

Her gaze dipped to where her food sat untouched. She dug into her purse and took out a twenty and slapped it on the table.

"No," he protested. "I've got this."

"I'm not your charity case. And neither is my mother."

He slumped in his booth as she swept out of the restaurant. His omelet was no longer appetizing, and now he had two of them. He almost got up to go after her and offer her a ride, but he doubted Kami Lee English—Preston—had lost her stubborn streak. She was too much like her dad.

CHAPTER 3

$\mathcal{K}$ami steered Ben's Saturn over the gravel roads that led to the hunk of flimsy trailer house she'd grown up in. Another yawn interrupted the trip. She'd gotten no sleep last night, stewing about the conversation with Travis the whole time. And the financial corner she'd backed herself into.

If Austin hadn't danced on all her insecurities when she'd brought up buying the empty store, maybe she wouldn't have blown up at Travis. Her mom might not be selling, but Travis had highlighted a problem. Eventually, something had to be done with the place, and the sooner the better, otherwise it could be a money drain. Money they didn't have.

How easy it would be to sell to the Walkers. They'd swoop in with a big "You're welcome" and work a mighty profit out of the place, all while assuming she and her mother were useless.

The placating look on Travis's handsome face… Her fist tightened around the wheel. She hated being on the receiving end of that look. Somehow it seemed worse because it was from Travis. Even after she'd slept with him and ran back to

Austin, believing what everyone said. *A man that smart was only interested in her for one thing, and he'd gotten it.* Who was she to think he'd want to stick around? But he'd treated her respectfully the few times they spoke before she'd moved. Until last night.

That place needs a lot of work.

She let out a disgusted sound. Like she didn't know.

"What, Mom? Did you say something?"

Kami glanced in the rearview mirror where her daughter's flaxen head was bent over the electronic device that might as well sprout from her palm. "You would know if you weren't buried in that phone."

Kambria lifted her brows in the *I'm not rolling my eyes so I can't get in trouble* way.

Ben's parents had bought her the phone, making it sound as if a responsible mother would've already gotten her one. They insinuated Kambria was in dire danger as she waited at home for a whole forty-five minutes after school before Kami's shift was done at the diner. She argued that her daughter had a phone, a small pay-as-you-go one that cost barely a cent to keep up. They'd insisted on a "reliable" smart phone.

And what Ben's parents wanted, they got.

Kami pulled into the mile-long drive that led to a rundown house nested in ratty trees. Somehow, Ben's parents and her mom got along excellently, leaving Kami swimming alone in well-intentioned waters. Her mom with a questionable reputation and a failing farm and Ben's parents with their Lexus and pensions had bonded over their young kids expecting a baby when they should've been deep into their freshman year of college. None of them had wanted her and Ben to get married, but he'd been the strong one in the relationship. Kami had gladly stepped aside and let him fight their parental battles. As the straight-A football player, his words had seemed to hold more credibility.

Unfortunately, an arrangement that had worked when he was alive failed her completely when he died. It wasn't that none of them took her seriously; they just lacked all faith in her competence and ability to accomplish anything.

They neared the house, and Kambria plastered her face against the window. "OMG, Mom. Grandma's tree fell!"

Kami's gaze flicked to the tree, an old willow that had shaded half the front yard and had been the best climbing tree ever looked destroyed. The ragged stump jutted about six feet off the ground, the heavy limbs piled underneath. Black mottled branches gave it an ominous appearance.

"It was really sick." If Ben were alive, he would've chopped it down and hauled it out. Anyone else would charge more than Mom could handle.

"Aw, that's too bad." Kambria's mournful tone made Kami smile. Full of attitude one minute, back to sweet little girl the next.

Kami parked in front of the house. The big garage ten yards away was full of crap her mom couldn't sell. Nothing useful, like a tractor that could haul big, round bales. Kami chewed the inside of her cheek as she pondered the possibility of buying this place.

Switching her future options from opening a gymnastics academy to ranching wasn't a natural transition. What did the two have to do with each other? Nothing, other than they both were huge parts of her life.

Buying the space for her gymnastics academy would leave her and Kambria in a tiny apartment while renovations were done. She'd have a lot of stress hiring and training coaches and building up class size to where they could support the facility. Learning to run a business was another huge hurdle, along with finding adequate fund-raisers and steady sponsors. The community was supportive, and she was a local girl, but she was still Earl and Pam English's daughter. A nobody born of nobodies with no credentials behind her name to give sponsors the warm fuzzies to hand money over. It had been a decision fraught with indecision, but she'd made it.

Then Travis.

Ranching was a business she knew. She'd helped her dad, which also meant she probably learned a lot of the wrong ways to do business. She'd been in gymnastics since she was four and she'd ranched just as long. The knowledge, the experience, to run a ranch was in her. Somewhere.

What she didn't have was the right equipment, the time it'd take to repair all the fences, or any livestock. But she had a job. Two, actually. And she could start small.

She and Kambria could move into this place while her mom could finally escape the gravel roads that clogged up so badly in the winter.

Kambria took off after the cat-size shadows disappearing behind the barn. Another reason why she didn't want to lose access to a place where her daughter could run like a kid and have animals.

Kami eyed the house she'd grown up in as she climbed out of her car.

She so didn't want to move back here. It had lacked character and any sort of special features beyond windows that opened when she'd grown up in it, and now it was just rundown.

Yes, getting her mom out of it was a good idea. Getting her and Kambria in it—not so hot of a plan.

Her mom came out onto the sagging deck. Mom was a little shorter than her without the muscle tone Kami had built up in her gymnastics career. Her blond hair now needed help to stay blond, but she looked much younger than fifty-eight. "Hey. What's up with you two for the weekend?"

It wasn't unusual for them to stop out, but Kami often called first. This was a conversation she wanted to have in person so her mom knew she was serious about her plan, no matter how impulsive it was.

"I ran into an old friend last night and he'd heard a rumor that you were thinking about selling."

Mom rolled her eyes. "Doc and his big mouth. He's stuck with an arm up a cows' behinds all day that I swear he loses his filter when he gets around real people."

"Why didn't you tell me?"

"Because I've been trying to convince myself it's a good idea. This is my home, Kami. It was your grandparents' home." She indicated all the land behind Kami. "Not even your dad could destroy it. I stayed out of pure stubbornness even though I was past the point of trying to start all over again."

"The Walkers want to buy it."

Mom snorted and crossed her arms. "Of course they do. It'd be perfect for them, and they'd probably try to point out all the reasons why my asking price is too high. As if they couldn't afford it."

"I can afford it," Kami blurted. So much for easing into the topic of her buying it.

"You can't be serious." Mom peered at her. "You are. Kami Lee Preston, how the hell do you think you can buy—" She straightened with a knowing nod. "Ben's life insurance. His mom has been asking if I knew what he'd had. She didn't believe her son's job wouldn't have come with a plan, but you never said anything. Not that you ever do," she muttered.

Good god, if she'd mentioned Ben left behind a three-hundred-thousand-dollar policy, then his mom would've "should" on her all over the place. *You should put it away for*

Kambria's college. You should buy a decent house. You should let us take care of the details.

They'd pelt her with their suggestions until she caved and turned control over to them. Just like they'd had with the burial, her old house in Normandy, and had started doing with Kambria.

They were the *real* reason she'd moved back to Moore.

"I had other ideas for it, but we need to save this place, Mom. Keep it in the family."

With a heavy sigh, Mom nodded. "I agree, but I won't be any help. One fall off a horse and my bad back is done. But I can't let you take on my problems. It'd just be selfish because I don't want the Walkers to have it. They have everything so damn easy. If they want to expand their operation, I ain't gonna bend over backwards to help them like everyone else in this county."

Kami didn't argue. She knew the feeling. The Walkers made everything look easy, always had. While her dad had raised his blood pressure to dangerously high levels stressing over fences and new gimmicks to make money. Those random ideas now clogged the barn, the Walkers rolled by with a new tractor. Or a new horse appeared in their pasture. Their trucks got bigger, and so did the smiles on their faces around town. Since Kami had moved back, she hadn't seen any change.

"Mom, it's not selfish to want to fight for a legacy. For the gift of passing land on to your grandchild. For the gift of a childhood that didn't include waiting at home alone in a small apartment."

"Land is one thing, but if you have the money, why not set it aside for Kambria?"

"I already have. I invested some." And that was before Ben's mom had started nagging. "But I'm more interested in creating opportunities for Kambria to grow. I want her to… I want her to see me doing something more than scraping to get by." *And I want to be able to talk to a man like Travis Walker and not feel like he's so far above me that I must look like a scavenging mouse.*

Her mom pondered her words. This. This was another reason why she'd moved back. Mom had her moments when she listened, really listened to what Kami had to say. Those moments were far and few between, like when Ben had proposed and Mom said that was the craziest idea she'd ever heard. Two eighteen-year-olds getting married and settling down without trying to go to school. It'd never work.

Kami had made it work.

Dammit, she'd make this work, too. And her mom took her seriously far more often than Ben's parents.

"Mom!" Kambria sprinted by. "A horse!"

She ran down the drive, her arms waving. A horse came down the ditch with a rider who swayed with the motions, his body relaxed, his head tilted so the brim of his navy blue hat blocked the bright June sun.

"Good lord," her mom muttered. "She's gonna spook the horse."

"No." She patted her mom's arm and infused a hint of sarcasm in her tone. "It's one of the Walkers. Their horses are just as perfect as they are, and I remember Reba. She's a calm one."

Kami didn't rush after her daughter. The rider was clearly Travis. She'd know the wide set of his shoulders anywhere. Beyond that, she'd secretly spied on him out riding when they were kids and her brain hadn't let go of the way he rode.

Travis wouldn't let anything happen to Kambria, or he'd politely excuse himself and nudge Reba away if he didn't trust his horse around her. Responsibility had been one of the many points of attraction she'd had with him.

Her daughter chattered excitedly, keeping pace with the

horse. Travis laughed, his gaze lifting. Kami swallowed hard. The man was much too potent in broad daylight. Kambria was holding her hands together, pleading with him.

Please don't beg him to ride. Kami held back a groan. The girl loved all things animal and had relentlessly asked about horses since they'd moved back. *We can ride now, right, Mom? Grandma has that land.* As if a tiny apartment was the only obstacle to owning a horse.

They approached with the crunch of hooves on the gravel drive.

"Tell you what," he said, his voice too deep for his own good. "You get your mom to sign off on it and you both can come out anytime planting's done."

Kambria blasted past him. "Mom, did you hear that?"

Ugh, it was hard to hold onto righteous anger when he was such a nice guy. "What are you doing here, Travis?" She kept the hostility out of her tone and barely managed to not sound breathy.

"I was taking Reba here out for a spin and I saw your car drive by. I wanted to check in."

That was not a warm glow that lit her insides. "Kambria, why don't you go play? Just stay away from the tree."

"But, Mom—"

Kami shot her the same look she'd just gotten from her own mom. Kambria's shoulders fell and she jogged to the shed where three cats lounged in the sun.

Travis whistled low. "That tree's done for."

Kami glanced at the remains of the willow. Reality seeped in. Her weekend to-do list just turned into finding any tools left in the garage or barn and tackling the massive limbs. Fuck, she'd need a chainsaw.

Get it, girl.

Somehow, her fierceness from last night had dwindled.

Travis tipped his head in greeting. "Pam." He swung down

from Reba. Kami tracked his long legs and the ripple of his muscles under his emerald green shirt and crisp blue jeans.

How did he not even look dusty? She'd bet that if she took her favorite Ariat boots out of the closet that she hadn't worn since she found out she was pregnant, they'd look dirtier than Travis's boots.

"How're your parents doing, Travis?" Mom sounded polite, but like she wouldn't mind hearing they ran into money troubles and were arguing constantly.

"Good. Lovin' Arizona." His sly smile was teasing. "But I think they just like to tell me how nice it is there when I'm plowing drifts of snow taller than me."

Her mom chuckled, her humor genuine. Was she like Kami? Wanted to hate the man, but he made it impossible. Damn Walker charm.

His gaze met hers, his smile died. "I'm afraid I may have spilled some false news to Kami."

Mom shook her head. "It ain't false. Actually, we were discussing that very thing. Kami's going to buy the place."

Kami sucked in a breath. Triumph didn't explode within her. This was happening. She was buying all the pastures and fields around her, along with the dilapidated out-buildings and feeble house. She'd be a business owner all right. Disappointment rose that she couldn't go back to coaching, wouldn't get the thrill off seeing her gymnasts in competition.

The magnitude of what she'd just agreed to settled over her. When the hell was she going to have time to do all this?

PAM'S ANNOUNCEMENT wasn't a surprise. Travis watched a myriad of emotions play across Kami's face. Her expression settled on muted panic.

She was going through with it then. It'd been a big decision between him and his cousins, but they'd decided they'd be fools not to jump on the sale as soon as it was listed. They'd even discussed meeting with Pam to get it going. By the time the sale was complete, they'd still have decent weather to get some things prepped for the next growing season when they could plant their own silage and start building a herd for at least one of the pastures—the only one Pam hadn't allowed people to store their junked vehicles in.

It was hard to be happy for her, but she'd gotten what she'd wanted. "That's great, Kami. I wish you the best."

Another flare of *oh shit what'd I get myself into* passed over her face. "Thanks."

The rest of his family would be sad to hear they'd missed an opportunity. He'd tell them that Pam had offered to Kami first, not that he'd spilled the news and Kami had jumped on it.

Her reaction wasn't what he'd expected. Smugness? No, that hadn't been her. An exultant smile and her strolling around announcing all the changes she'd make, maybe. Kami had been a headstrong child. The champion on the school bus when older kids targeted the younger ones. She told everyone how it was going to be and charged ahead. Other kids had naturally followed her lead.

Hell, he would've followed her anywhere. He had, too. Until she'd run back to Austin-fucking-Anderson's arms after their brief night together.

She wasn't quite the same Kami from those days. It seemed like they'd each lived a lifetime since then. She had a daughter who wasn't so little anymore, and just like Kami at that age, she was spinning cartwheels through the grass.

Mom lightly tapped her arm. "I'm going to start lunch since you and Kambria are going to be hanging around all weekend messing with that damn tree." She wandered back to the house.

Reba puffed and nudged him. She wanted to get back to grazing, but he didn't want to leave.

Kami turned a disheartened smile on him. "Thanks for stopping by. That was really nice of you to check up on me."

About that. He hadn't ridden horse for weeks until this morning when he was struck with the urge to not just ride, but head through his own pastures to the ditch running to Kami's place. Checking on her wasn't just an excuse. Wanting to see her again fueled that excuse.

Her little girl looked like her. He remembered Ben from football. She had his height and his eyes, but her mischievous grin was all Kami's. So was her athletic ability, apparently. His eyes widened as she went from being upright to falling back to bridge.

"Holy shit," he said.

Kami's grin morphed into proud mom. "She's getting good."

"Taught by the best, isn't she?"

"I'm running out of equipment. I don't think a beam would fit in my place." Her smile faded as she glowered at the tree. "Well, I'd better get to work."

That was his cue to leave. He had a lot of work to do. He really did. There was the…the…

Fuck it. "I'll ride Reba back and grab my chainsaw."

Her brows rose, but he didn't miss the flash of hope. "No. The tree's not your problem. I've got it. Didn't you say you had planting?"

He'd get out of it. "Not this weekend. It's no problem."

He gripped the saddle horn and propped his foot in the stirrup. Swinging easily into the saddle, he glanced down. His mouth quirked. Was it wishful thinking, or had she checked him out?

Her gaze shifted to the tree. The massive limbs would need nothing less than a chainsaw.

"Really, it's not necessary." She didn't sound convinced.

"I know." He tapped Reba's flank and flashed Kami a grin as his horse sauntered off.

He'd finagled himself an entire weekend with Kami. The cost was back-breaking work in the hot sun, but worth it.

He'd earned a degree in restraint by the time Reba reached his house. The mare's health was as important as his own, otherwise he'd run her through the ditches. To get back into her own pastures, she would've willing worked herself into a lather.

Reba was brushed and back grazing before he went in search of tools. He fired up his truck, attached the flatbed trailer, and pulled up to the tool shed. The Quonset and barns were for tractors and livestock, and all the guys had their own set of equipment. He ducked into the shed and located what he'd need.

The chainsaw got loaded, along with a two-gallon gas can, a reciprocating saw, an axe, a sledgehammer, and a wedge. Work gloves went into the cab with hearing protection and safety goggles he grimaced at. There had to be something better. He searched and finally found glasses that looked like clear sunglasses. Better. Just because he was a geek didn't mean he had to look like one.

He glanced down at himself. Running to his house, he crashed inside and changed into his work clothes—beat-up jeans and a long-sleeved Carhartt pocketed T-shirt. Satisfied he was as protected as he could be, he rushed back to Kami's place. The drive felt as long as the horse ride.

When he pulled in, she and her daughter were tugging and pulling at loose branches. They'd formed a nice pile with just them and a large pair of clippers.

Lining his truck and trailer next to the pile, he killed the engine and hopped out.

Kami stopped with the eight-foot branch she was hauling. "Since you didn't take the hint, where do you want me to load this?"

He set about getting his gear on. He seated the goggles on top of his head and hooked the ear protection around his neck. He stuffed his hands into the work gloves. "Where you've got it. I'll break down the trunk and large branches. We can stack the wood in the bed of the truck and pile the branches on top. Do you want to keep any for firewood?"

She slanted a look at him. "We don't have a fireplace."

"Fire pit?"

"Dad always used an empty barrel. It's probably shoved in that barn somewhere." She jutted her chin toward the decaying structure with the faded, weather-worn wood that displayed little of the red paint from its prime. "It's a lost cause, don't you think?"

"Most definitely. What we'd discussed was getting everything out of there before the next major storm toppled it and we had to dig it out."

She nodded, her expression resigned. "Dad left some useful things behind, but there's pure junk in there, too. He collected anything he thought would be worth money, then never sold it." Her gaze switched to the pasture, her mouth pulling into a frown. "Kind of like those cars. But I think Mom got the money upfront."

Yeah, Kami would have a full-time job for weeks just hauling old cars out of the pastures. With the right equipment and enough helpers, it'd take a few days.

"Give me a shout when you tackle those, too. I'd be glad to help."

Kami stared at him. Behind her, Kambria had seized the

break in work to twirl through the yard and do a cartwheel thing that lands like a flip. Just like her mother at that age.

"Why are you helping me, Travis? I cock-blocked your business expansion."

Just his work, not him. He stared across the field in the direction his property lay and answered as honestly as he could without saying he was still crazy about her. "Because I can't imagine anyone else owning my house. I would've had a hard time forgiving my parents if they had sold it out from under me."

When his dad and four uncles sold the Walker Five farm and ranch operation, he and his cousins had all been in good places in their life. And they'd had each other. Kami had her daughter, who could run a push mower and was probably big enough to drive a riding lawn mower—if Kami owned one. The barn or garage could be hiding one, but now that he was close enough to see the piles of crap bulging against the door, it'd take weeks to sift through the stacks to find a mower underneath.

And Pam had probably sold it if it'd been any good.

She clapped the dust off her hands. "I can't let you do it for free."

The stubborn stance was back. His mind spun to come up with a deal that wouldn't cost her money. "Food. Lunches and dinner. I'll do breakfast tomorrow before I come back."

She put her hands on her hips. He forced his gaze to stay on her face, not where her shirt pulled against her breasts. "That's not an even trade."

She'd never tasted his cooking. "Then I'll take the wood, too. We can burn it during our family parties. And we like to have a stash on hand in case a blizzard knocks out power."

"I thought you Walkers would all have generators."

"It's always good to have another backup during our winters."

She shoved her hair off her face. Kambria was running toward the barn, chasing a cat. Kami glanced at him, then back to her daughter.

"Deal," she said before she rushed off. "Kambria. Stay out of the barn!"

He followed, more out of curiosity. What had Earl done with that thing? No wonder he'd struggled with a dwindling herd if he didn't have a good winter pasture and a barn to bring sick calves to rehab.

Kambria stopped her trek. "I know, Mom."

"Yes, you know, but I don't want you playing close to it, either. Do you hear that creaking?"

They all went quiet. The wind was only ten miles an hour, but faint groans emanated from inside.

"Fine." Kambria dropped her head back and trudged away. Abruptly, she spun around. He jumped, but Kami didn't flinch. "So did Travis talk to you about the horse ride?"

"Kambria," Kami groaned.

Travis chuckled. He could've high-fived Kambria for bringing it up. "Absolutely. Since I'm taking the weekend off, why don't we go when I finish tree clean up?"

"I couldn't—"

"I have a horse for you, too," he interrupted. "She's not a barrel racer, but I think you two would get along."

"Mom used to barrel race," Kambria broke in.

"I remember," he answered and grinned at Kami. "You have to promise not to challenge me to a race."

Kami playfully scowled at him. "Then don't ride past my practice ring and tell me what I'm doing wrong."

He'd only suggested a few changes to her technique and within minutes they were lined up in her back forty, horses snorting, sensing the tension. He'd lost that race by more horse lengths than he could count.

If Kami had listened to him, she could've taken first at the

Fourth of July rodeo. But she hadn't, and it'd been her last race.

Was it how he said things that drove her off? Or did she become defensive when anyone gave her advice?

"Fine," Kami muttered again. Kambria whooped and twirled off. Kami shot him a bemused expression and peered into the barn.

The door hung open, only attached by a bottom hinge. Must and old metal aromas wafted out. When she braced her arms on the frame and leaned to squint inside, he couldn't keep his eyes off her shoulders. Her peach tank top molded against her body, exposing defined muscles in her arms and shoulders. The way her thighs filled out her jeans, he wouldn't be surprised if she joined Kambria doing cartwheels and bridges.

She pushed off the door, muscle rippling through her shoulders. "I can't even. So much work. I'm just going to worry about the tree first."

Her hips swayed in her faded jeans as she made her way to their weekend project. He followed, content for the first time in…years.

CHAPTER 4

The next day, Kami once again parked at her mom's place. Kambria burst out of the car, racing to tell her grandma that tonight was the night she'd get to ride horse.

Her daughter had taken the disappointment well the previous night, but Travis had toiled for hours on that damn tree until the sun set. She'd packed lunches and made last night's dinner in her mom's place. After that, she'd had to begrudgingly invite him to her apartment for tonight's dinner. The creaky folding chairs and card table at her mom's wasn't big enough for all of them, and cooking a real meal was hard when the oven cooked unevenly and only one burner worked on the stove.

Kami had needed a night to talk down her hormones. Watching him, stripped down to a snug T-shirt, wielding a chainsaw like a boss, and flinging hunks of wood like they were soup cans left her needy and uncomfortable in a way she couldn't remember. Even as a lust-filled teen looking for attention in the arms of insincere boys, she had known her reactions were superficial. It wasn't until deep affection had grown for Ben and the respectful way he'd treated her that she'd realized there was more to sex than physical pleasure.

But memories of her one night with Travis, and the way he was helping her now, threatened to confuse her good sense. She had to remember that he was only helping her because…she hadn't figured that part out yet. Was he seriously interested in her?

Her stomach fluttered. No, it didn't matter. They'd been leagues apart as teenagers and time had only increased the gap.

She gathered the cooler that contained their lunch and got out. She still owed him a meal since he'd had to leave.

The front door to the house creaked open and Mom came out. Travis wasn't here yet. Kami waved to her and went to the garage and threw open the overhead door.

Her heart sagged at the sight of the overfull garage. Why'd Dad have to collect so much shit? If she thought there was anything in there that was worth money, she'd call *American Pickers* out here and give away everything.

Setting the cooler around the corner out of the sun, she straightened and assessed the piles with a critical eye. How much could the dump handle and how many trips in the pickup would it take?

Would her old pickup even start?

Mom's footsteps crunched behind her. "Kambria said the Walker boy's coming back here."

Walker boy. He was twenty-eight. If she remembered right, his birthday was a month before hers. His mom had always sent the best cupcakes to school. Even when they weren't in the same classroom, he'd always given her one on the bus.

"Yes. We're trading food for labor."

Mom snorted. "The boy don't want your food. What are you doing, Kami?"

"I'm trying to come up with a plan of attack for this garage."

"I'm not talking about this dump. I'm talking about Travis. I'll be honest, he's always been a nice kid. Respectful when his parents weren't. But if you start with Travis, you're taking on his whole family."

Kami crossed her arms. "I'm not starting anything with Travis. He's just helping."

"I don't want him using you to get over his fiancée."

"What's that supposed to mean?" Moore was full of single women who'd go Fight Club over a chance with Travis.

"Doc said he heard from Bunny—you remember their cousin who's a vet, too?—that he goes to help Michelle's parents all the time. He's like a son to them, and since their boy lives across the country, they've really come to depend on Travis since their daughter died. He commented to Bunny that the emotional loss aged them like twenty years."

"He and I aren't anything." No one could ever get over the loss of someone special, but he wouldn't use her. He'd never been that kind of guy.

Then Mom ruined her mood by saying, "He's certainly better than all them other boys you put out for."

Kami jerked around, making sure Kambria wasn't nearby. "Why is my history always getting thrown back at me?"

"Because I'm afraid you're going to repeat it."

"I've only dated Austin since I've been back."

"Exactly."

Kami barked a laugh. "Don't worry. Austin and I aren't seeing each other anymore, and I'm not interested in seeing anyone else. I have a daughter to care for, and now this place. I don't have time for a man."

The rumble of an engine came down the drive. The thrill

of getting to see Travis was overwhelming. She was going to have to resist all offers of his help if she was this bad off.

Her mom's stare burned into her. "Make sure you remember that, just like you make sure to remember that his family never once offered to lend a hand when Earl died. I think they were waiting for me to give up so they could swoop in."

Those dark days filtered through her memory. The quietness had been the most notable. No one stopped by with food or paper towels and napkins. Three pews in the church had been filled for the memorial service. Then silence. Weeks later, she and Mom started loading cattle for sale.

Travis parked by the remains of the tree and waved at them.

"Your *help* is here," Mom murmured as she brushed past.

Travis climbed out and swaggered toward them in all his farm boy glory. Tall, with his navy blue hat and a matching shirt so snug she could count his abs, his long strides quickly ate up the distance between them. No one could guess he'd worked a fourteen-hour or more day yesterday.

"Mornin', ladies." His easy grin warmed her in more places than she wanted to admit. He nodded to her mom before his bright gaze landed on her. "It should go quick today."

Kami could only agree. He was hard to be around yesterday when she'd had frustration and desperation fueling her, but on a fresh day, she'd likely start simpering and batting her eyelashes.

"Let's do it, then." She hadn't meant to bark the order, but she could not get her hopes up about whatever was between them. The only relationship that took priority was her and Kambria.

Travis ducked his head, his expression serious and jogged

to his truck. Her mom shot her a warning look before stomping off.

Kami worked by Travis's side for hours. Sweat rolled down between her shoulder blades, and she threw her hair up in a ponytail. Travis never complained, but steadily hacked at the giant limbs, cutting them to size. His biceps when he ran the chainsaw…

She swallowed hard and spun around to load more limbs, only to find them all done.

So it was either stare at Travis more or eat. When the saw went quiet, she called to him. "Hungry?"

"Sure, let me wrap this up."

Wow. That whole tree was gone. A part of her childhood cleaned out. Like her dad. One night he was there, the next morning he wasn't. And neither had anyone else been around. Sure, Travis had been a kid then, but his parents hadn't. One more reason why she shouldn't hope for more with the man. His family was probably worse than Ben's, thinking she could do no right and trying to run her life.

None of that. Ever again.

Just get through the horse ride for Kambria, feed her weekend lumberjack one more meal, and then she was done with him. She had to be.

KAMI HELD BACK on her loaner horse while Travis, astride Reba, kept close to her daughter. They ambled through newly hayed pastures. Rolling hills and fence-line stretched before them. A soft breeze carried the scent of the wild-flowers that lined the ditches. Travis said they'd stick to the pastures so if Kambria fell, there wasn't a road or fence so close.

"Mandrell's the horse we use to break everyone in," Travis

said to Kambria. "Crystal Gale has a little more spirit. That's why your mom got her to ride." He grinned over his shoulder and winked at her.

"This is sooo sweet." Kambria giggled.

Well, there went Kambria under Travis's spell. He hadn't had any trouble charming her daughter. But none of it seemed to be an act. He seemed to genuinely enjoy her company and her incessant chatter. His laughter at all the questions were full of good humor, and all this after hours of wrenching work.

Remaining emotionally distant when she could finally relax and let the smell of horse sweat and fresh air seep into her bones... The days of jumping on a horse and cruising to the nearest pond were long gone. God, she'd missed that. How had she not remembered how much it'd been a part of her life?

Because there'd been no other choice. Couldn't afford cattle. Needed money instead of horses. There was a baby to raise, bills to pay, in-laws to keep from breathing down her neck.

This life... Hard work rewarded by nature. She could get used to this again. Wanted it for her daughter. Wanted to find love again.

Kami looked around. Where had that thought come from?

Now that it was out, she couldn't take it back. Yes, she wanted to spend her life with someone. A man who was as good to her daughter as Travis. Only not Travis.

Could it be Travis?

The murmurs about her and Travis had been too...self-affirming. *What was he doing with her? Didn't he know he was too good for her? Think she's only into him to get help with her homework? What do you think they even talk about? You know he's not with her for her brains.*

Just because more than eleven years had passed didn't mean anyone's opinions had changed. If anything, they'd gotten worse as the golden boy riding next to Kambria, patiently teaching her horsemanship, had only endeared himself more to the community.

Her mom said he had his Ph.D. in… Geez, she couldn't even remember. Agriculture something. If she couldn't even say it, what the hell would they talk about?

Kami slouched in her saddle. The problem was that she didn't want to just talk with him, not after a day of watching his body move.

They meandered the perimeter and made their way back. Kami stretched her back and adjusted her position. Crystal Gale nickered. She patted the horse's neck. She was younger than Mandrell, but Kami doubted she'd spook easily.

She closed her eyes and let her body sway with each step, soaked in what she was fighting for by buying her family's land.

Her eyelids floated open, her gaze landing on Travis. He cocked a brow as if to ask if she was okay. She gave him a small smile.

For a few seconds, everything was more than okay. Her girl got to experience a tiny bit of the life Kami wanted for her.

"Mom, can we do this next weekend? Oh, wait. I'm with Grandma and Grandpa."

There wasn't a cloud in the sky, but her world darkened a few shades, like it always did when Ben's parents were mentioned. The tug-of-war between them about what was right and wrong for Kambria wore her down.

"Just give me a call whenever you two want to go." Concern flickered in Travis's gaze. Damn, had he seen her reaction to her in-laws?

"Sounds good," she answered with as noncommittal of a tone as possible.

If he noticed, he didn't show it. His grin was back in place. "What's for supper?"

"Brussels sprouts." His grin fell, and she chuckled. "Just kidding. I planned something quick and easy, but filling. It's Kambria's favorite actually."

"Tater tot hotdish." Kambria pumped her fist in the air.

Kami grimaced; a sense of shame bloomed. The Walkers ranched, and each and every freezer they owned was probably filled with the best cuts of beef in the world. All she could offer was ground beef covered in canned cream of mushroom soup and mixed veggies. Planning it after the first day's exhaustion of tearing apart the tree had happened because it was easy. She should've ran to the store and gotten something...better.

"Well, if it has Kambria's approval, it must be good. I just have one question. Does it also have cheese?"

Relief poured through her so fast, her mouth stretched wide in a grin. "Is there any other way to make it?"

He put his hand over his heart. "Thank God. Michelle was —" He cleared his throat and looked away. "She was lactose intolerant and I missed my cheese."

She should tell him that would happen, that his lost love would pop into conversations like she wasn't gone and it'd feel awkward because of the worry that the other person felt awkward.

"Mom puts in lots of cheese, Travis. Don't worry." The awkward moment almost passed when Kambria asked, "Who's Michelle?"

Kami waited for the answer. How often did he get that question in a town where everyone knew who she'd been?

He stared straight ahead. "She was a very good friend of mine. She died from an aneurysm the March before last."

"Oh. My dad died suddenly, too. Car accident."

His shoulders tightened. "I'm sorry. That, uh, that sucks."

"Yeah, it does."

They rode quietly together, their horses in sync.

"I really like Mandrell," Kambria announced. The awkwardness drained away and they were chatting about horses again.

But they reached his barn and that meant that she and Kambria would head home and throw in dinner. Travis Walker was coming over.

TRAVIS RINSED THE LAST DISH. He hadn't meant to polish off the remainder of the casserole, but it had been hot and filling and cheesy. He almost groaned again. Kami played it off like it was no big deal, but she didn't make an open and dump casserole. She seasoned and added things that made it as irresistible as her.

During his time with her this weekend, he'd gotten glimpses into the adult Kami.

How envious he'd been of Ben Preston. Travis had fantasized for years about being the one she ran off to marry. Would she have gone to college with him? Would *he* have gone to college?

Logically, he knew it wasn't meant to be. He wouldn't have been able to support her any better than her husband had, and it seemed like he'd done a fine job. Rather that Kami had flourished no matter what—at least until he died.

Travis witnessed her expression when Kambria mentioned her grandparents. Was there trouble between them? Resentment? Did Kami get lonely when her girl was gone?

What look did he get when someone asked him about

Michelle's parents? Guilt? Did it look like he carried the weight of their farm on his shoulders? They'd been afraid of losing him and to help himself move on from what his intentions had been when she'd passed, he'd ensured that they didn't feel like he'd traipsed out of their life.

After the funeral, his cousins had taken over some of his normal duties while he'd helped Phil plant. Then harvest last year, he'd harvested from sunup to sundown for three months straight. The only time he'd quit was traveling between home and their farm outside of Fargo. During the winter, he'd moved snow off Michelle's headstone and repaired any equipment Phil had neglected. Running the farm had fallen far from Phil's priorities since Michelle had passed.

"You didn't have to stay to do dishes." Kami reached around him for a towel. Her breasts brushed his back. A light touch he possessed too much awareness for. Blood pooled in an unfortunate area.

How had he kept his erection at bay all day? If he hadn't been so tired last night, he would've had to take care of business himself. He hadn't had to do that for years, and not just because he'd been in a relationship.

Kami stuffed the last dish into the dishwasher. "Be right back."

She disappeared around the corner. Kambria had flounced to her room after the meal and they hadn't heard from her since. Travis hadn't had to say anything all through the meal. The girl had gone on and on about her riding experience. She only stopped talking horses to fill in all of her mom's gymnastics resume for him—as if he hadn't been an avid follower when he was younger.

He shoved his hands into his pockets.

The kitchen was a small box, with an equal size dining room. Her bedrooms were probably just as small. The living room was slightly larger. The whole flat could fit into his kitchen/dining room area.

She appeared with a bemused expression. "She's passed out on her bed. On top of the comforter and everything. It's like sleep took her by surprise and knocked her out."

He chuckled and leaned against the counter. "I'm sure you've been told, but she's a good kid."

Kami smiled, her expression almost shy. "How are Brigit and Justin?"

He only had one word for his younger brother and sister. "Vexing."

"How so?"

"Justin went to school for international marketing and he lives in Denver but travels the world. He doesn't call, doesn't give us any details. Mom likes to brag, and I swear she's going to put a tracker in his phone one day. Brigit was applying to med school and Mom's certain she'll get in. I think she's even lined up a job in Phoenix for her. She's probably lined up a job in Phoenix for Justin and that's why she's so pissed."

"All three of you, done with college?"

He ducked his head. "Pretty much. Brigit graduated in May, but she refused a party. Like I said, Mom likes to brag and that didn't go over well. But they're all coming back for Dillon's wedding in July."

"Sounds like you all give them enough to brag about."

He pushed off the counter and stalked her. She took a step back. Then another. "You make it sound like a bad thing." Coming to a stop closer than he anticipated, he didn't move away. His hands twitched to brush her face. Was she as soft as he remembered?

"It's a good thing, but it just shows that even though we grew up next to each other we're worlds apart." Her head was angled to look up at him, the look in her eyes dejected.

"I'm just a man, Kami."

Her gaze dipped to his chest, then back to his eyes. "You're never just anything. None of you are."

He had no clue what she meant, but those lips of her beckoned him. He dipped his head. Her mouth opened in a hushed gasp. Softly, he touched his lips to hers.

Plush, hesitant. Just like their first and only night together. He wouldn't have guessed she'd be timid then. The young Kami blew through life like a force and took what she wanted. She'd been a cheerleader, a barrel racer, and her in a gymnastics leotard had tormented all his teenage hormones.

But now she was a woman, and he'd meant what he said. He was a man. A simple farmer.

Increasing pressure, he rested his hands on her waist. One of her hands snaked around his neck, the other gripped his shoulder.

He could spend the rest of the night just like this and be content.

He swept his tongue out. Would she let him in?

When she opened for him, it was like an early Christmas present. She was as savory as the dish she'd made. Hugging her closer, he deepened their kiss. Everything around him faded, all he had to concentrate on was them and he was going to make it count. Kami English—Preston—was back in his arms. Could he keep her this time?

His mind whirled. What would he do next?

An idea took shape until he almost grinned. Twirling with her tongue and tilting his head, he flattened his hands along her sides. They were going no further tonight.

He'd been aware of her reputation when they were younger, but he hadn't cared, just wanted to be the man she ended with. He didn't like to repeat what hadn't worked before and jumping into the backseat with her at his first chance had somehow driven her away.

So he was going to take his time. And if he wasn't going to take it further than this kiss, then he was going cherish it for as long as possible.

She skimmed both of her hands to the front of his chest, then glided them under his arms and around his back. Her breasts were smashed between them. He wanted nothing more than to palm them, test their weight in his hand. But he craved her taste more.

Take it slow.

"Mom? Mom!"

Kami ripped out of his arms and spun around, her hand to her mouth. Travis staggered back a step, but recovered and shit—he had an erection. Playing it as cool as he could, he went back to leaning against the counter, propping his body at an angle. He kept his expression as pleasant as possible, anything but the raging lust he'd been experiencing just seconds ago.

"Kambria. You're awake."

He couldn't see Kami's expression, but it had to look as guilty as her tone.

Kambria gave him a hard look. "What are you still doing here?"

Whoa. The bright, cheerful girl he'd been around all day was gone. In her place was a territorial daughter who didn't like seeing her mom with another man.

"Don't be rude," Kami admonished, hand on her hips. His hands had just been there. Was her shirt still warm from his touch?

Nope. Not going there with the tiny militant glaring at him.

"You're right. I've overstayed my welcome, but it's hard when your mom's so nice to be around." He lowered his voice and tried for a conspiratorial whisper. "Even when she makes me work all day."

Kambria harrumphed, but her mouth twitched. He'd take it. Leaving on a good note with Kambria was more important to him than he'd thought.

He crossed to Kami and lightly set his hand on her shoulder. Her startled glance betrayed her surprise that he was so forward with her in front of Kambria. He hoped it was the correct gesture. While it was awkward to be caught by the girl, he didn't want either of them to think what had happened was shameful.

"I'll call you later." Maybe if he acted like this thing between them wasn't done yet, Kami would believe it. He dropped a kiss into her hair. From the corner of his eye, he saw Kambria's brow raise, but no hostility stained her face. "When you two can come out and ride again, give me a ring."

"I don't…" Kami crossed her arms and turned out of his reach. "I don't have your number."

"I'll call you then. Maybe next weekend?" He was aware of Kambria's avid gaze jumping between them.

"I work extra shifts at the bar on the weekends I'm alone."

Kambria snorted. "Yet you find time for Austin."

Kami bristled and she shot Kambria a warning look. His stomach plummeted. He'd been naïve to assume that imbecile was out of the picture. What did she see in him?

"You. Go to bed." Kami jabbed her finger in the direction of the girl's bedroom.

Kambria stomped away. The one takeaway Travis got was that she disliked Austin. He wanted to fist-bump her.

Kami spun around to him, her features tight, her face full of determination. "Good night, Travis."

Her abruptness disturbed him. Something was bothering her, and it wasn't just getting busted by her daughter.

"I'm sorry. I didn't realize you and Austin were still…"

"We're not anything," she snapped. Her features softened, tinged with regret. "He and I aren't… Not after the other night. We tried when I got back, but the warden in there doesn't like visitors."

"Maybe it's the visitor." Her gaze popped to his. He shrugged without remorse. "If no one's told you, you can do better."

"I did do better, and look what happened."

All his ambition drained out. She wasn't over her husband. Here he'd been devising a slow and steady way to romance her when she was still grieving. And of course, what would everyone else say? Did they all think he was supposed to be grieving? No one knew he'd fallen out of love with her—and that was what made this thing with Kami irresistible. It felt more powerful, deeper, more real to him than what he'd felt in a long time.

The connection he had with Michelle was very academic. They bonded over classes, talked shop all the time. But she'd had no interest in the aspects of his life that made up his very being. Sure he had a brain, initials followed his name, but farming wasn't just what he did, it was who he was. His hobby developing farming and ranching games, was just that —a hobby. Because he'd been home alone all night while Michelle had stayed in Fargo. When he had gone out, the night ended early because his cousins had found someone to spend the night with. As they started settling down with significant others, they'd gone out less and Travis had been alone more.

The words to ask her out again were on the tip of his tongue, but he swallowed them down, saying instead, "I had a good weekend. I mean it when I say that if you need any help, call."

"Thanks, Travis."

Before he left, he grabbed his phone and found her number. He hit send. Her phone vibrated on the counter. She twisted to frown at it.

"There. Now you have my number."

"How'd you get mine?"

He smiled, and heat from earlier in the evening fused into his look. From her gaze stuck to his mouth, she noticed. "Despite what you saw this weekend, I'm not all muscle."

With a nod, he walked out, her soft chuckle echoing after him.

CHAPTER 5

Ten more miles and they'd arrive at Normandy. Kami loosened her hand around the wheel. This weekend's hour-long trip to her former in-laws pumped more dread through her than normal. They were going to find out that she was trying to buy her mom's land. And they'd have an opinion. They always had an opinion.

She managed to keep her intentions under wrap. If her mom hadn't told anyone, and Travis hadn't told anyone, then it was still between the three of them. But Kambria was the wild card, and if she spilled a secret, she'd also backtrack and let out that she'd been asked not to say anything. Then Ben's parents would lose trust, thinking Kami was keeping secrets from them. For her daughter, she strove to keep a smooth and open relationship.

Kambria thumbed her phone off. "So what will this family reunion be like?"

"You'll get to play with your cousins." Ben's sisters had moved out of state and Kambria rarely got to play with their kids. "Some of your dad's aunts and uncles will be there. You'll play games, and—"

"I don't understand why you won't come."

Because I wasn't invited. "I'll pick up some extra hours. I didn't know your dad's family very well." Because they hadn't been interested in knowing her, just her daughter. And she wasn't working at the diner or bartending. She was grabbing her work gloves and heading out to her mom's.

"Has Travis called yet?"

She glanced in the rearview mirror. Kambria lacked all the mutinous attitude she usually had when she asked about Austin. Actually, she never asked about Austin. Must be the horse riding that gave Travis extra points.

"I missed his call earlier this week."

"Did you call back?"

"No," she answered evenly. "I've been busy."

They approached the modest ranch-style house of her in-laws. Ben's dad was outside mowing the lawn. He shut the mower off and waved.

Kami parked. Kambria rushed out, throwing her grandpa a wave and running into the house.

Forcing a smile to her face, she got out. Ben's mom didn't come out and greet her. That was nothing new. She chatted a few minutes, then moseyed back to her car, trying not to seem too eager to leave.

Finally, she made it home. She gathered her phone and wallet and trudged inside.

Glancing at the screen, she fumbled her items. Shit, she missed Travis's call.

Her belly clenched. Should she call him back? What'd he want? She could easily pick his brain about what the Walker Five had planned for her property. They could meet for a bite to eat. Or he could come over.

Justin was an international whatever. Brigit was going to be a doctor. Travis was already a different type of doctor. His mom liked to brag. And one time, she'd overheard Travis's dad ask hers if he'd been to STU. Stupid University.

She stood, chewing her lower lip and staring at her phone in her palm.

She dumped everything on the counter and went into her room. It was time to do her own research.

~

"Hi, Kami. I'll be out repairing some fence on the northwest pastures, so if you need a hand, just let me know."

She hit replay.

"Hi, Kami. I'll be out repairing some fence on the northwest pastures, so if you need a hand, just let me know."

Before she'd crawled into bed, she'd swung out and grabbed her phone. Now it was morning, and she hadn't budged from her warm cocoon.

She hit replay. Each time Travis's voice rumbled her name, an uncoiling in her belly threatened to move south.

She wasn't accustomed to sexual frustration. After Ben died, she hadn't been interested. Then, after her move home, she'd started thinking about an identity that didn't revolve around being a widow and well, there was Austin. Single as always. At least he made sure he was single when she was willing.

That was one redeeming trait with him.

Why was Travis so willing to help her? She wasn't so desperate that she'd take him any way she could get him. She didn't want to be his stepping stone, or worse, his regret that he'd settled. Why would a successful, intelligent businessman slash scientist be interested in her?

Sex.

She'd almost scaled Travis's body and latched onto his tonsils when he kissed her.

She frowned at the ceiling. The kiss was splendid. But she started unraveling her misgivings behind the action. The reason why Ben had appealed to her in the first place.

They had their fling through football season, he kept asking her out, and when her pregnancy test had a plus sign that might as well have been ten feet tall, he'd been so thrilled. They'd have deep conversations about raising kids, future aspirations. It'd even been fun to pick names with him. He insisted on using a spin-off of her name and since a combination of their names didn't work, they'd settled on Kambria. And that was the thrill of Ben.

A hot tear rolled out of the corner of her eye. Lazy Saturday mornings with him, discussing what their weekend plans were…cooking breakfast together…taking Kambria to the lake. Their life had revolved around their child and included a stability she hadn't known before. For the first time, she experienced a relationship that wasn't all about sex.

Ultimately, that was why Travis was off limits. He might be smarter than her, he might have more money, but if he thought sharing her bed was the start of a solid relationship… Well, she deserved better.

TRAVIS WIPED sweat off on his shoulder as Cash positioned the wire, the last on at least a football field length of fence they were repairing. Since they formed the perimeter of the bull pasture, they wanted to ensure it was as secure as possible. He clamped the wire after securing it around the post.

"Finally." Cash took of his hat and wiped his brow. "It's a hot bitch out here today."

"At least there's a nice breeze." Travis tossed the tool into the box and dug out his phone.

Blank screen. He scowled and tucked it back into his pocket.

"Dude, is there a hot commodity update on the price of wheat?"

He glowered at Cash. "We didn't plant wheat this year."

"No kidding?" Cash said sarcastically. "We could've shaved an hour off today if you weren't stopping to check that damn thing all the time."

Travis clasped the top of the metal post and put his other hand on his hip. "You and Abbi fighting or what? Or are you two menstruating together?"

Cash flipped a finger up, surprisingly not his middle finger. "One, I don't make those jokes around her. Pussy jokes about the cat are a go, PMS jokes—no-go. I learned the hard way." He looked like he was going to say something, but instead bent to collect all the items scattered around the rectangular toolbox.

"Talk to me, Cash."

"It's nothing, man."

Cash chewed on the inside of his cheek. Travis gave up and was turning away when he spoke. "Your mom called me the other day."

"What? Why? Is something wrong?" Travis talked his heart rate back down. Dillon was getting married this summer and Cash was getting married in the fall. It was likely a wedding question that Travis would be clueless about.

"No, not that at all."

"Good. Good. Then why are you reluctant to tell me?"

"She's worried that you haven't mentioned dating again."

Travis bristled. "And?"

"She said she'd like to see you bring a date to the wedding and asked if I knew anyone."

Travis gritted his teeth. Mom was hoping to take advantage of Cash's womanizing past. "Aw, hell. I'm sorry, Cash."

Cash shrugged it off, but his shoulders were tight. Yeah, he'd been insulted. "I get it. They aren't here to see how I've changed. Anyway, I told them that no fucking way was I getting involved in your love life."

"Verbatim?"

"I'm not stupid. But I was clear that I was not going to set you up with anyone."

Travis sighed and rolled his neck. *Why, Mom?* He'd be mildly irritated if he hadn't run across Kami. But he had, and he wanted things to progress naturally, without pressure. What would Phil and Della think when he started dating? They were barely surviving without Michelle. Their son wasn't around. What if they felt they were losing him again?

He scrubbed his face. Truthfully, Phil and Della were a major reason he hadn't been interested in dating. He dropped his hands and his gaze landed on an old rusted pickup towing a flatbed trailer bumping along in the neighboring pasture.

Kami's mom was never out in the fields. Had she tracked him down for a reason?

Cash pushed off the tailgate. "When'd Pam English get a trailer?"

"Right? When'd she get anything new?" She certainly wouldn't start now. Was she actually going to help her daughter?

"I can't believe Kami thinks she can turn that mess into a working ranch. I guess we'll have to wait another year or two for her to figure out she needs to sell."

"What makes you so sure Kami is going to fail?"

Cash scoffed. "When has that girl stuck with anything in her life?"

Travis shot him a glare. "People change."

Cash raised his hands in defense. "Sorry. I forgot how you were about her." He dropped his arms, and they watched the pickup veer off to the mound of scrap metal. The profile in the pickup wasn't the weathered grimace of Pam English but an intent young woman with a swinging ponytail.

Kami had her mom's truck and intended to tackle the scrap pile. By herself? Was she going to drop the trailer and go back for some kind of heavy equipment to help her load any of that?

"Travis?"

"Hmm?" But Cash didn't elaborate. Travis glanced at him and scowled. "What?"

"Are you…interested in her? Dude. I don't need another round of trying to cheer you up every time you see her with another guy."

Travis ran his tongue across the front of his teeth. *Don't lose my temper.* "She's not like that."

"I wasn't saying that. Fuck, Travis. Me, of all people, know better than that. I was talking about how she dropped out of rodeo after her dad died. How she jetted when she got pregnant, then rebounded back when her husband died. I'm talking about how when her situation gets rough, she gets going. And turning that neglected acreage into something not only usable, but profitable, is going to be rough to say the least."

When Cash said it like that… But he still didn't know Kami. He was older than them and thankfully, she'd been wrapped up in Austin during the years Cash was exploring the wonders of sex.

"She deserves a chance. It's her home."

Cash shot him a look. "That place isn't fit to be a home for anything." He ambled to the truck and climbed inside.

Travis turned to follow, but stopped. He twisted back to look at Kami. She'd gotten out and was wandering around the piles of old cars. He couldn't make out her expression, but it had to be hopeless.

He jogged to the pickup, opened the passenger door, and grabbed his water bottle and lunch bag. "I'll see you later."

Cash draped an arm over the steering wheel and cocked an eyebrow.

"She deserves to have a little help. She's lost a lot and she's trying to save what she has left."

"And you two are going to throw an entire car frame from the seventies onto that trailer?" Cash blew out a sigh and rolled his eyes toward him, then back out the windshield. "Dammit, fine. I'll swing by Aaron's and grab the loader. But what the hell's she going to do with a fully loaded trailer?"

"I know. I'll talk to her." He shut the door and slapped the frame. Cash drove off.

Travis threaded his way through the pasture. He reached the newly repaired fence and carefully separated two rows of wire to wedge himself through. Kami had disappeared between two old cars. As he got closer, her mutters grew clearer.

"What the hell were you thinking, Mom? Dammit, this is such a mess. What the hell am I supposed to do with all this shit?"

He rounded the fender of an old Chrysler. "Hey, there."

She shrieked and spun around. He jumped back before she started swinging.

"Travis! I thought you guys left." She recovered quickly with a stern expression and her hands planted on her hips.

A smile played over his lips. She was so out of her element. "Cash went to grab the loader."

He scanned the mess around him. The sun peeked behind

a cloud, throwing shade over them. A metallic smell tinged what should've been a lovely open-field scent. He inhaled deeply. Pam must've at least had the previous owners rip out the environmental hazards before they towed their junk here. He detected no undertones of oil or gas.

"What do we have?" he asked.

"*We* don't have anything. I have my mom's bad decisions to clean up."

"Kami—"

She shook her head. "This is not your problem."

The sun escaped its block, the bright light making her eyes shine like a stout ale. She squinted at the sky and abruptly stomped to her truck.

He stayed on her heels. "It's not, but we were ready to clear this out anyway."

The truck door screeched as she ripped it open. She dug around inside, giving him the sweetest view of her rounded ass in her worn jeans. A hat was in her hands when she popped back out. Shoving it on her head and threading her ponytail through the opening, she scrutinized him.

He was transported back fifteen years to when a young Kami rode horse with her dad to his house so their parents could argue about some perceived grievance on her dad's part.

She crossed her arms, making her plain gray T-shirt bond with her cleavage. As if the last week hadn't been hard enough to talk his body down from, this image was going to cost him sleep.

"The thing is, Travis, eventually I have to learn how to save my own ass."

He ruminated over that. She had a point, but it didn't negate all the obstacles she faced. "I get it, but how are you going to do this all with a trailer?"

"I'll load what I can and dump it before I have to get the

trailer back. This'll give me a good idea of what equipment I'll need."

"Wait, the trailer's rented?"

She nodded, a guarded expression overtaking her determination.

"So you're paying by the day."

She nodded again.

"And you're okay leaving this sit in your yard and paying until Monday?"

"Of course not. It's going back today."

"They close at one."

She blinked and glanced at the trailer. "No, he assured me he's open until four today."

"Not the equipment rental place, the scrap yard."

Her mouth dropped open. A delicate line formed across her forehead. "Then I guess I dump it tomorrow."

He hated heaping bad news onto her. "They're not open on Sunday. Don't you work all day Monday? Because they're only open until five."

She nodded, her eyes glistened with a hint of moisture. Dammit. Did she feel like he was attacking her, proving how she wasn't cut out for this?

"None of us do this alone." He kept his tone soft, encouraging. "Cash'll be here in a half an hour and we'll cherry pick what we can. It's only ten. I bet we could even get a trailer full or two to the dump. And while you return it to the rental store, we'll load up one of our trailers and I'll just go Monday and get rid of it. This pasture will be checked off."

Her lips formed a stubborn line. For a moment, he feared she'd turn him down. "Isn't he bitter about your missed opportunity?"

A shadow crossed his face. "There'll be another one."

"I guess that'll work."

He'd rejoice, but she probably gave in because the cost of

keeping the trailer until she could unload and return it next Saturday terrified her. The amount of money she had squirreled away was likely dedicated completely to this endeavor. And yeah, he thought her chances were slim, and that made him resolute about not wasting her money.

He smiled. "Great. Now, what do we have?"

CHAPTER 6

Kami stood several yards away from the loader as Cash and Travis maneuvered the last hunk of old car onto a flatbed. Exposed earth and dead grass outlined where all the junk had been for years. Her next project was to tackle the top half of a school bus in the adjacent pasture. Her dad dragged it out there, claiming it was a shelter for calves, but it was an eyesore.

The car was placed. She stepped in to secure it down. Cash backed the loader away. Travis waved him off. The drone of the engine faded into the distance as Cash took it back to Aaron's. Travis said he'd keep the scrap pile loaded and drop it off in the morning. She had an hour to trade vehicles at the house and run home to meet Kambria when her grandparents dropped her off.

Spending her weekend with two of Moore's most handsome farmers shouldn't have left an uneasy pit in her stomach. But the evaluating looks Cash gave her and the tense way he interacted with Travis left her wondering what was between them. Did it have to do with her? Did Cash know about the kiss? Was it her reputation?

She didn't know Cash very well. He'd been a couple grades ahead of her and had his own stories told about him, but from what she heard, he'd settled down with an out-of-town girl. Was he all righteous because he'd been tamed and now the focus was on her?

Her phone rang. She shucked her gloves and dug it out of her pocket.

Ben's parents? "Hi, Martha. Is everything okay?"

"Hey, Mom!"

Some of her foreboding drained away when her daughter responded instead.

"Hey, sweetie. Are you on your way back?"

"Um, no. That's why I'm calling. Can I pretty, pretty please stay another six weeks?"

"*Six weeks?*"

At her shout, Travis dropped the anchor straps he was tightening, his expression concerned.

"Grandma saw a flyer for this cool gymnastics camp for the summer. It starts tomorrow. Can I? It's right in town and you'd save money if I don't go to day camp."

No, she wouldn't save a dime. She'd have to keep paying or lose Kambria's spot.

"I can't, honey…" Six weeks. Without her daughter.

"But, Mom, you always say how you wish the gymnastics academy didn't shut down in Moore so I could go."

Kami chewed her lip. She and Ben had put Kambria in gymnastics lessons as soon as she was old enough, but that ended after he died. She was teaching Kambria what she could, but their living space was too tiny for a cartwheel, even a front roll. And she refused to do anything more without the proper padded equipment.

If it was anything but gymnastics… When the rest of her life had fallen apart, her mom had managed to afford lessons.

Then when she'd moved to Normandy to be with Ben, she'd worked part-time as a coach.

It was almost like Ben's mom knew exactly how to manipulate her into keeping Kambria for the summer. They'd never had this much tension between them when Ben was alive, but her in-laws resented her moving.

"I really don't know," she began.

"Wait, here's Grandma. Bye, Mom."

Martha came on the line. "Kami, it's a really good opportunity."

For who? "I don't want to be without my child for the summer."

"Of course not, but you're so busy and she has the whole house here to roam in. And…she told us about the farm."

Kami squeezed her eyes shut. Of course she had. "That's between me and my mom."

"Oh, I wouldn't want to intrude." Martha's uber reasonable tone always made Kami feel like a petulant child arguing with her. "If she was here, it'd give you extra time to work."

Kami opened her eyes to stare at the ground. "Not really. We'd be here on the weekends no matter what."

"I'm sorry, I just knew how much you loved gymnastics and how highly you spoke of it…and how proud Ben was when Kambria did her first somersault."

There went the dagger in the heart. That man had been ridiculous over his little girl. "Fine, but she has to come home on the weekends, and you'll need to drive her."

Good, Kami. Keep it up. Don't the let the MIL push you around.

"Absolutely." A beat of satisfaction swelled until Martha continued. "Oh, but there's the trip to Itasca we promised her in two weeks. And in a month, we said we'd take her to the Mall of America."

Kami ground her teeth so hard, Martha had to be able to hear it.

How could she? She'd planned this whole damn thing. Kambria would only be around six days out of the next six weeks and if she said nay, she'd look like a complete, ornery bastard.

"Fine. Have her back by five on Friday." She clicked off before Martha could say another word.

Aw, shit. She hadn't said the full goodbyes and I-love-yous to Kambria.

Her hand fell limp, phone loosely clutched. The backs of her eyes burned.

No crying!

A tear fell.

Broad shoulders blocked out the sun. "Hey, hey. What's wrong?" Travis brushed the tear away, but another quickly followed.

"My manipulative mother-in-law figured out a way to get Kambria to stay with her until August." A sob escaped. She hadn't been without Kambria for so long; it was her and her daughter against the world. But it felt like her girl jumped ship at the first opportunity. "I already told Martha no when she brought it up last spring, but suddenly there's this fantastic gymnastics camp—" She snarled and stomped away.

He was right behind her. "And if it was anything else."

She whipped around and almost ran into his solid chest. "I know, right? Ben loved watching her in lessons, said he couldn't wait to watch her perform at halftime shows like I used to. That devious hag knows how much I love that sport and uses how much Ben loved that I was in it against me." Pressing the heels of her hands against her eyes, she released a gusty breath. "Whatever. It's done. I caved. I'll have to use the extra time to work here."

When she lowered her hands, she met his gaze.

Was he going to kiss her? Her pulse kicked up.

"Want to come over and I'll show you my hard drive?"

"Um…"

He grinned, flashing the dimple that was only visible when his full smile was in use. "I designed a game. It's an app, really. For the phone."

"You design games, too?" Her heart sank. Was there anything he couldn't do? Any other ways to prove how he was too good for her? "I'd better get home."

She stepped around him. He swiveled around to follow her. "I have a hidden agenda."

That made her pause. "And what would that be?"

"You make edible food."

If a way to a man's heart was really through his stomach, she'd been on the wrong path for years. "I do, but it's not hard. It's all edible."

"Not once I get my hands on it. Whaddya say?" He was smiling again, only he was adding the heat he had in his eyes last weekend. "I have ingredients, but they don't metamorphose into something good if I touch it."

She thought it over, all the reasons why not. The top of her list was that he used words like metamorphose and that he created games.

He interrupted her mental checklist. "You kinda owe me."

"For what?" She glanced at the bare patch of pasture that he and Cash broke their backs to clear. "Oh."

The money from the scrap metal sat in an envelope in her truck. They'd refused to keep it no matter how much she insisted. The rusted metal that the scrap yard didn't take the guys had hauled to their place to drop at the dump tomorrow. She owed them. A lot.

"I don't know if I can cook that many meals to pay you back for all you've done."

"You can start with this week."

She stared at him. Had she heard that correctly? "This week for what? Making you food?"

A thrill went through her. Seeing him every day? The way he dressed down for manual labor in faded Wranglers and a flannel shirt that she wished he'd shed, but of course he didn't or he'd cut his arms up loading scrap. His ball cap was grungy and frayed, his work hat. She felt better knowing he wore normal working people clothing. He could wear his typical crisp button-up and sharp blue jeans and do all this without getting a speck of grit on him and she wouldn't be surprised. Travis Walker had always seemed to function at different standards than she did.

Her gaze swept the loaded flatbed. "I don't think a month of meals would be enough."

"How about the full six weeks?"

Her eyes flew wide. Six weeks was a long time. How could she argue? *Please, help me all weekend with your own equipment and when you ask for any kind of reimbursement, I'll turn you down flat.*

Did she even want to argue?

"Deal," she said before she could disappoint herself forever. The opportunity flooded her mind with more benefits. "I'll throw in dessert if I can pick your mind about the tasks I need to accomplish here."

One thing this weekend taught her was that she couldn't do this herself. Not at all. The Walkers didn't do it themselves and, yes, they had a ton more acreage than her and both farmed and ranched, but there were five of them, not to mention their parents' well of knowledge and any other cousins who were around to help.

"Deal." His lopsided grin tugged at her like an invisible line. At times he seemed to orbit in a galaxy much more organized than hers. But then he smiled like that and he was the geeky kid on the bus who fielded homework questions while she giggled with her friends over lip gloss.

Six weeks. Eating with Travis. She couldn't read more into it.

What if he tried to kiss her again?

~

TRAVIS ROLLED the tractor next to the Quonset that housed the combine. Kami's car sat in the driveway loop, closest to his house, pointing out like she needed a getaway. Planting would be done this week. Then he needed to find something more active, maybe start jogging in the morning with Cash and Dillon. He had zero self-control around Kami's meals.

She was a decent cook, even she admitted her food was nothing spectacular, but that didn't matter. He hadn't been kidding when he said his culinary skills were lacking. They lacked in all ways. From burning his damn toast to finding mold in his jelly if he did conquer the toaster. He'd lived in the dorms for longer than necessary and half wondered if he'd gotten his graduate degree just so he could justify eating on campus.

Michelle had been fantastic in the kitchen, but she'd always wanted to eat out, sampling the eclectic mix of bars and grills popping up all over Fargo. She reveled living in city limits. One of the many reasons why she wasn't going to move to Moore. One of the many reasons why they argued—because he wasn't leaving Moore. It was his home. Always had been, always would be.

His parents had moved to Arizona, his brother and sister matured into their own lives, only he was left to run the legacy left behind by his grandparents. Well, him and four of his cousins, but he wanted to. Farming was in his blood. Ranching was the fun hobby on the side. He was outside, working with his hands, moving his body, and during his down time when he wasn't at a fire pit with his family, he could play on the computer. And that's all it was. Play.

Michelle had kept bugging him. Why didn't he go for an IT job? Fargo was hopping with a technological boom.

He designed a farming game, instead. She hadn't even told her family. So, he hadn't told her that he could buy a new laptop from the earnings on his game in the first six months it'd been out. Nothing spectacular, but not an epic fail in his book. If he hadn't sold one game, he'd still be proud of himself. His parents sure were.

What had driven him to show Kami? As soon as the offer left his mouth, he went with it, willing to endure the fallout, hoping his weekend of being a good neighbor would win him points.

She'd clapped her hands in delight and immediately downloaded the app on her phone. They'd spent so much time hunched over his computer, she'd only had time to assemble sandwiches, his meal du jour. But they tasted better when she made them. Then she'd interrogated him about his food likes and dislikes.

After two days of toiling next to her in the sun, watching sweat glisten along her slender muscles, spending an evening so close to her without touching her had killed him all night long.

She'd arrived Monday evening as he'd ambled into the yard on his tractor. By the time he'd filled the hopper back up with seed, she'd whipped up a batch of spaghetti with meat sauce. Then she'd left to work at her mom's place.

Tuesday, she'd had chicken enchiladas ready by the time he stepped into the coolness of his house. She'd even made an extra batch to freeze, with heating directions across the top. Then she'd left to work at her mom's place.

She repeated the scenario yesterday and now it was

Thursday and her daughter would be back in town the next night. He had five weeks left of meals. Did he make it clear that what he really wanted to taste was her, spread out on his table, or his bed, or on his floor. He didn't care. The memory of that one night together over a decade ago was enough to revert his adult hormones to those of his needy teenage self.

She'd been so responsive. Just like her kiss the other night. She'd melted into him.

He had to stop. Planting his hand on the warm metal of the tractor, he closed his eyes and dragged in a deep breath. Take it slow. Romance her. That was the plan.

It was a shitty plan.

No, it was the grand plan. Only the timeline had been moved up because Dillon's wedding was the end of July. Oh, he could tell they were still waffling, but if he secured a date, they might have more confidence that he wasn't a lost mess.

He wrapped up his duties. The tractor was ready for the next day. He jogged back to the house. Burning off the cold pasta he had for lunch, which packed way more of a punch than his typical cold cut sandwich.

Letting himself into the house, he let the rightness settle into his bones. Kami had the code. Sounds of spoons scraping pans and savory aromas wafted from the kitchen. Coming home, to this house, to a person he enjoyed spending time with was a long-held fantasy come true. It'd been a dream he'd held onto so tightly that it'd stalled one relationship and prompted him to wonder if he really was better off being a bachelor.

Like the other nights, he went to the bathroom to wash up first. He found a fresh shirt that didn't smell like dust and sweat and changed. His pants would be all right, otherwise he might scare her off if it looked like he was dressing up for her.

Why couldn't he make another move? Because his first attempt had ended awkwardly.

An arrogant side he didn't know he possessed thought it should be a slam dunk. They'd grown up together, had already been together, and were reconnecting years later when they were both tragically single. But she wasn't jumping into his arms. She resisted his help and sped out before dishes were even dry. The deal about the land might be what was fueling her, but what if she genuinely didn't care for him? Had their one night together been a one-sided fireworks show? She'd walked away, and that shouted at him that yes, it was.

But the way the fire raged between them during that short kiss... No, he couldn't believe she wanted nothing to do with him.

He inhaled deep but couldn't identify the smell emanating from the kitchen. Strolling in, he found her bent over the counter, thumbing through her phone.

"Hey. What's on the menu tonight?" he asked.

She jerked her head up and clicked out of whatever program she'd been in. Her phone disappeared into her back pocket.

"Knoephla soup." Her no-nonsense tone made it seem like it was just another meal. An ordinary soup.

His groan came straight from the well of wanting his stomach had been living in since he'd moved back home to be cut off from campus food. "Have you tasted the grocery store's knoephla? I could live off that stuff for a week, but I never get down there quick enough. The damn pot is empty by the time I get there."

"Do they make it homemade, or heat and serve?" Was that a hint of challenge in her voice?

"I'm so deprived of quality food that it makes no difference to me."

He crossed to the cupboard to collect bowls and cups. Sometimes she had the table set, but whatever was on her phone must've occupied her time. Setting the table was the least he could do. The deal was she'd cook in return for his help, but he hated walking in and sitting down like she was supposed to serve him.

When he turned with his hands full, she was staring at him, her expression incredulous. He lifted a brow in question.

"I have one more question." When she crossed her arms, challenge written all over her face, he asked, "Do you make your dumplings from scratch, or buy them?"

"Well, I'll have you know, Mr. Walker, that I can make a double batch cheaper than buying one bag of precut dough. It's just flour, salt, and baking powder. Add water, and voila."

She shooed him to the table and came behind him, bearing soup.

As much as he wanted to chat during the meal, he couldn't. The food was too good, down to her admittedly packaged freezer breadsticks.

When he was scraping the last vestiges of his bowl, she set her napkin on the table.

"Don't worry, I'll clean up," he said before his last bite. She'd been intent on doing everything to level the field between them, but it was getting late. She put in just as full of a day as he did.

"Actually…"

His excitement spiked. She wanted to stay longer?

"I was hoping I could bribe you with dessert if you helped me outline a plan for Mom's property."

He set his bowl down, held his expression at deadly serious. "What kind of dessert?"

She narrowed her eyes, but her mouth twitched like she

was trying not to smile. "Banana cream pie. Not at all home-made, unless you count adding milk to the pudding powder."

Why'd he have that third breadstick?

Because they were haying tomorrow and he needed the energy. That excuse worked every time.

"Leave the leftovers here and I'll show you what I already had written up."

She was mid-rise when she stopped. "You've already made an outline?"

He nodded. "It functions as a timeline, too."

She straightened and stepped away from the table. "Of course it does."

He watched her go. Any hint of intimacy they'd developed over their meal and short bursts of conversation was wiped out. What'd he say?

Kami flopped the pie on the table. It bounced and whipped cream smeared the flimsy plastic cover.

After her late-night research, she had an idea of what tasks she should put on her to-do list, but Travis had it freaking printed out already. With a timeline.

It was nearing the end of June and she hadn't even asked around about who could hay the land. Or if any of it was even good for haying. As a good daughter, she should at least arrange for a rancher to hay it and sell them the bales at a discounted rate for doing the work. The money would go to her mom until the sale was finished. How long had it been since any of that acreage had earned a dime?

Her confidence didn't get bolstered from being in Travis's place, with his bookshelf full of textbooks in alphabetical order. And his library full of references and rows of magazines, all ag related.

Flyers from equipment dealers and seed companies lined his end tables. Reps from the company must bang down his door. Getting Travis to sign off on their product gave their company the Walker Five account.

She rummaged through a drawer for utensils when a shadow fell next to her.

She screeched and jumped. Spinning around, she threw a hand up. It landed on Travis's chest. He held his hands up in surrender.

"I'm sorry. Sorry." He didn't step back, and she left her hand right where it was. "I wanted to see if you needed help, or ask if anything was wrong."

Her shoulders sagged; her hand slid down his solid chest to fall at her side. He towered over her, but she didn't mind, not when he looked so concerned about her.

When was the last time a guy worried about her? It'd only been Austin since Ben, so the time had been the morning Ben had died, when he'd promised to stop for milk and lunch-meat before he came home from work. She'd had a full evening of coaching and hadn't had time to pick up anything for supper between school pickup and work.

Locals gossiped that she'd only married him because he got her pregnant, but that wasn't it at all. Being a single mother hadn't intimidated her then, and it didn't now. She'd fallen for Ben because he'd been a good man. Like Travis, he'd obviously been infatuated with her. Unlike Travis, she hadn't assumed he'd grow bored with her and rush off to bigger and better things.

Ben would've moved from Normandy to the ranch. Then they'd have raised Kambria on the slice of paradise, most definitely with horses. It wouldn't have mattered that she and Ben had nothing more than a push-mower and two snow shovels. But he was gone and she was on her own, floundering.

She puffed a lock of hair out of her eyes. "Nothing's wrong."

His expression said he didn't believe her.

"Yeah, okay. I feel so incompetent around you."

He recoiled. "Me? Why?"

Said like he really didn't know. Was he book smart and not people smart? That made Kami feel a little better.

"You're a doctor."

"Ph.D. type. Not medical."

She threw her hands up. "You're also really talented. At farming. At ranching. At computer shit. At business. I was afraid of being beholden to you even more than I am by asking for your advice and here you have it all written up, organized, and set in a timeline."

He propped one hand on the counter next to her and his other hand on his hip. She was partly caged in by a hot guy with brains to match his looks.

"I'm the same geeky kid you rode the bus with every day. I just like to be organized and I get bored easy."

Exactly. Bored. She'd never have the intellect to keep him. "You weren't geeky."

"Nerdy?"

"All the girls had a crush on you. All of you Walkers." She'd only wanted Travis and as soon as she'd had him, she'd known they were never meant to be. Everyone said so.

"I wasn't into all the other girls. I had eyes for only one."

"Please," she scoffed. "I bet they lined up outside your truck for…" She gulped. What they'd done together inside of his pickup had been magical. She hadn't known what an orgasm was before Travis.

He lifted a shoulder in a shrug. "I got asked out, but I kept hoping you'd give me another chance."

Warmth infused her and mixed with melancholy. "You'd have never stuck around. We have nothing in common."

He considered her for so long she started to squirm. "Did you and Ben have a lot in common?"

"Yes."

"What was it?"

Her defenses rose. "We're both from small towns. We both liked sappy movies and action flicks. We both…" Damn, there was more. Why couldn't she think of it?

"You both liked spending time together?"

She gazed up at him. "Yes."

"I didn't have much in common with Michelle. She's the only person I've been with besides you."

Seriously? A guy like him, with his body, had only had sex with two people? She'd had more experience than him by the time she was seventeen.

"We both enjoyed school," he continued. "That was what drew us together. She liked city life, I didn't. She liked sherbet, and nope." Kami's mouth quirked. "She was uncomfortable in my big family get-togethers and I think I'd be a hermit without them. But we still worked…for a while."

"What do you mean—"

He cut her off with a kiss, stole the rest of her sentence, seized control of her mind. She went from wanting to interrogate him on Michelle to wanting nothing more than to keep touching him.

He crowded in and wrapped his arms around her. The kiss deepened. The pie was forgotten. She was pressed against him from head to toe. Every cell in her body demanded that she never move away from him.

Desire like she'd never known before swamped her. It'd been too long since she'd been intimate. That had to be why her sex thrummed with her heartbeat.

Did she care what the reason was? Or that Travis was here, and she could do something about it?

He burned a path from her mouth, down her neck, while he untucked her shirt from her waistband. Why had she chosen blue jeans and not a wispy pair of shorts?

She gave herself free rein, roaming her hands up his shoulders, loving how they bulged and flexed, up to his trimmed hair. The slight curl in it had always driven her wild. It ran through her fingers like silk, so soft compared to the hard body against her.

He freed her shirt and splayed his hands along her sides. The flick of his tongue at her neck made her suck in a breath of delight.

God, that felt good.

His head jerked up, and he claimed her mouth again.

Yes, she needed this. But she couldn't go through another two weeks of after effects of nothing but a kiss. He wedged his knee between her legs. Friction. Yes, please.

Rocking into him, she groaned. She'd never been so ready to get to the act as she was now.

His arms flexed, like he might be trying to sweep his hands up to her breasts, but they were pressed too closely together.

No time for that! She released one hand from his head and guided his arm down until he cupped the juncture of her thighs. Just a little release. To keep from being painful.

Teasing her with his tongue, making her think he wasn't going to go further, he did nothing but alternate pressure and easing up.

A needy mewl left her. She should shove his hand away so she could ride his leg.

But slowly, he skimmed up to her waistband and undid the clasp. Without having to maneuver them into a new posi-tion, he wedged his hand between them into her pants, under her panties.

His low moan echoed hers as his fingers parted her folds. She knew she was wet, but the ease he teased her clit with— he affected her more than she'd thought. It was like her body was transported back to the new and powerful sensations he'd given her, when he'd shown her what sex was really supposed to be like. When he'd worshipped her body. He'd spent hours on her pleasure.

Since it'd been two minutes, did that mean he was as desperate for her, too?

She'd worried about earning back her reputation for being easy, but with Travis she didn't care. He hadn't bragged then, he'd likely show the same respect now.

This was just between them.

His tongue licked along hers as he spread her with his fingers and circled her nub. She gripped his shoulders and rocked into him.

He increased the pressure; another needy moan escaped. His other arm still anchored them together, otherwise she'd be bent back over the counter, smashing the pie, so she could bare herself to his masterful touch.

Widening her stance, she circled her hips, coaxing faster movement from him. Her orgasm was careening around the corner and it promised to hit hard.

He did nothing more but keep the same steady pace, matching the rhythm with his tongue, until she was holding off her climax just to enjoy the climb.

How did he make a frenzied act so slow and sultry?

The effort of keeping her release at bay took its toll. She broke their kiss and tipped her head back, her breaths coming in pants.

He blazed another path with his lips down her neck, the faint scratch of five o'clock shadow heightening the ecstasy. With slow precision, he moved his hand enough that one finger speared her.

She shattered. Crying out, shuddering, riding his hand. She didn't know how long it went on. He didn't move; she was the one going wild.

Dragging in lungfuls of air, she finally pried her grip off

his shoulders. He lifted his head, his hand still cupping her mound, but he must know how sensitive she'd be.

She met his gaze and stilled. Desire shone from his clear blue eyes. Pure, unadulterated. He was in no rush to seek pleasure for himself; he seemed to revel in being the one to cause her orgasmic bliss.

"Travis Walker, you always amaze me."

His lopsided smile snaked around her heart. If he'd had a cocky grin, she could defend herself. But he was sweet, earnest. Like that first night when he'd seemed so damn delighted to be able to make her climax not once but three times.

Why had she walked away from him again?

Right. Because she didn't want to see his back leaving her for not only someone else's body, but their brain, too.

"You've always amazed me, Miss Kami Lee Preston."

The sincerity in his voice didn't affect her. Oh, it did, but not as much as his use of her married name. Austin always pestered her about keeping Preston. *Keeping his last name ain't gonna bring him back.* She suspected it only reminded Austin that she'd moved on from him, if only for a short while. Preston stayed for so many reasons. She hadn't felt the need to change it back. It was her daughter's last name and always would be. And it distanced herself in other people's minds from the footloose girl who could only ace gym class. That was only important to her for Kambria's sake.

Travis captured her mouth again. A thrill rose, and it was as if her orgasm hadn't happened. She wanted him again, only much more than his hand.

She stopped their kiss long enough to murmur, "Travis, I want…" She flicked open the button of his jeans.

"Whatever you want, I want."

Their foreheads were pressed together, his arms held the

counter on either side of her. She felt safe in the circle he made. She worked his fly open and shoved his briefs down.

Her breath *whooshed* out. She was accustomed to coming back home and thinking everything seemed smaller through adult eyes. But Travis's erection didn't fit that category.

His thick shaft bobbed into her hand. She wrapped her fingers around him. His eyes drifted shut, his hips rocked. The tip glistened. She used the wetness to slide her hand around him easier.

"When you touch me, I can't think straight." His warm breath brushed her cheeks.

He can't think properly? "I can't believe your mind gets frazzled."

He groaned and tilted his hips until his shaft slid back, then he thrust back into her grip. "Around you? Always."

"I can't believe I intimidate you." Truly unbelievable.

His hips swayed. They both watched as she worked him without effort, enjoying the coiled strength under her palm. Velvet wrapped steel and searing hot skin.

"How can you not? You're stunning." He paused to catch his breath, the muscles in his shoulders quivering. "Your body is a work of art. I used to sit transfixed during your half-time routines. I only played to make sure I didn't miss Kami English flip across the court." He dragged in another breath and let out a growl. "I'm not going to last long."

"I don't want you to," she whispered. His words were flattering, but she wasn't that girl anymore.

"But it's really your smile I'd kill for."

She yanked her gaze up. His hair was mussed, his intense gaze now on her lips. After what they were doing, he was going on about her smile?

"Yeah," he panted. His thrusts quickening. "Your smile lights up every room, makes me feel like no one else is around, like you and I might— Oh, *Kami...*"

She tightened her grip. Like they might what? His hips jerked and he threw his head back.

"Kami!"

Hot release coated her hand but she didn't care. The way he growled his climax, the way his neck thickened with corded muscle, the way he called her name. He made her feel like they might have a chance.

He sagged into her, his arms coming around her. She released him and embraced him in return.

After a couple of minutes, he shifted his head enough to whisper in her ear. "Now that we have that out of the way, I can take my time with you."

She fisted the material of his shirt. He'd said that back then and he'd meant it. Memory flooded her body, heating her core.

She licked her lower lip. "We can start by taking your shirt off. It got a little messy."

His phone rang.

She relaxed her hands, waited for his reaction.

"Fuck 'em," was all he said.

She giggled, expecting that reaction out of his cousins more than him. Probably where he picked it up from.

The ringing stopped.

Travis pulled back enough to stroke her cheek. "Can you stay?"

What should be the worst idea in the world sounded divine. She worked in the morning, but what was one day working through lack of sleep. He'd make it so worth it. "Yes."

His phone rang again.

He hissed with frustration and jerked his phone out of his pocket. One glance at the screen and all hints of passion left his expression. "I'm sorry. I should take this."

Stepping away and turning his back, he answered in a low tone and strode out of the room.

So that was that.

Scanning the kitchen, she decided what she'd do. Wait here like the desperate sex-crazed woman she was, or have a piece of pie?

"No, it's fine. I'm not busy." Travis sidled into the den and pinched the bridge of his nose.

He'd only been at the precipice of an experience he'd been dying years for. Kami was in his arms again. There was something between them. She tried to keep her emotional distance and after tonight, he suspected why.

For a woman as spectacular as she was, she lacked confidence.

He could get past that. Whatever he had to do.

Michelle's dad, Phil, spoke, dragging him out of his lustful thoughts. "I just… We haven't…"

Travis sighed as quietly as possible. They needed room to grieve and whenever they talked to him, he felt like he only reminded them of everything they'd missed. Michelle wouldn't be getting married, or giving them grandbabies, even if Travis had broken up with her. She'd been an attractive, intellectual woman. He had no doubt she would've carved out the life she wanted for herself. But to her parents, all that would've been with him by her side.

"We wanted you to know how much we've appreciated your help."

"It's not a problem. Honestly."

It would be, eventually. Travis couldn't help run two farms over an hour apart from each other, but he'd have to suck it until Phil started emotionally recovering, or retired.

"I'm sorry I haven't called the past few weeks."

"No, no. You've been busy. Planting season, I understand."

"Do you need any help? Did you get the corn in?" Cash would step in and take over for him if he had to leave town.

"We're fine, son. I scaled back, like you suggested." Phil cleared his throat. "Maybe we should try to get together sometime? Della thought we could stop out there. You've been doing all the running."

Travis glanced at the door and caught himself. He hated feeling like he was hiding Kami, but he didn't want to add to their burden. "Sure, you're welcome here anytime."

"We'll give you a jingle when we're out and about next."

Travis bobbed his head even though the man couldn't see him. Calling first would be good. He'd hate to be out in the field when they arrived. Or caught with his pants down, his dick in Kami's tight fist.

"Call whenever you need to, Phil." Travis hung up, then hung his head.

His respect for Phil was boundless, and the fact that he called robbed Travis of the elation he'd felt with Kami. His resolve to take it slow lasted days, but felt like forever.

He hoped she hadn't left.

He glanced down. His cock was still hanging out, flaccid. All blood had drained from him when he'd seen "Phil" across the screen of his phone.

He tucked himself back in. Zipping up before he sported another erection just recalling the moment he released into her fist, he left his shirt hanging out to cover any residue left on his pants.

Had she cleaned herself up? Did she have regrets? Did she have hopes for more? He certainly did.

Everyone commented on his intelligence, but his wants were simple. The love of a good woman, surrounded by family, in the house he was literally born and raised in.

He had two of those things.

Leaving the den he called for her.

"At the table," she replied.

The flush in her face hadn't left. The pie on her plate was half gone, and a second piece sat in his spot. They hadn't even cleaned up from supper.

"I think you already gave me dessert."

The blush darkened and she took a measured bite. When he thought he'd pushed too far, she threw him a flirty look.

He dug into his piece. "When do you want to go over the list I prepared?"

"Kambria's home this weekend." She frowned. "You remembered, right? That I couldn't make supper this weekend?"

"Absolutely."

"I'll be working at Mom's as much as I can. You can catch me there."

He'd catch her anywhere.

They finished their pie in silence. He desperately wanted to ask her to Dillon's wedding and his intuition said it was too soon. But the wedding was in three weeks and if he waited too long, she might back out at the short notice.

They cleaned up side by side. He asked about her day, like he did every night. She rarely talked about it. They were just jobs to her. Her tone was dead and her face lacked animation if he got anything beyond "fine." Not like when she talked about her mom's place.

"You're still welcome to stay," he offered.

He consoled himself with the regret in her eyes. "I have an early morning but I—" a hesitant smile lit up her face, "— enjoyed myself tonight."

"Good." He resisted giving her a smoldering kiss. It wouldn't stop there if his lips landed on her again.

He walked her out. The night had cooled, the nocturnal sounds of frogs filling the air.

"Listen," she said and paused, looking around. "No motors. No one hollering to anyone else. No neighbors revving their engines. Just birds and crickets, and frogs in your ditch pond."

"I've threatened the frogs several times. We have a noise ordinance out here." He shot her a teasing grin.

She smiled and opened her car door. "Good night, Travis."

He watched her drive off, her taillights disappearing beyond the trees rimming the property of his home.

Well, he hadn't scared her away yet. If only he knew what'd he'd done last time. He'd meant to romance her this time, but she scrambled his best intentions.

Shoving his hands in his pockets, he wandered back into his house. Clouds of bugs swirled around the yard light and the light outside his door. He'd probably have three mosquito bites before he got back inside.

She'd admitted she liked what they'd done together. The optimism Phil's call had deflated bloomed again.

CHAPTER 8

Kami sat on her couch and grinned to herself as she read Travis's message wishing her a splendid weekend with her daughter and to let him know when she was able to meet about his write-up.

Determined not to let him do all the brain work, she'd outlined her own plan, one radically different. But once her research had touched on it, it all made sense. Would it make any bit of sense to Travis?

Her confidence wavered. She waffled on whether she should show him, or just listen to what he had to say. He had the big degree in this business. He had the experience.

She had neither.

Ben's parents hadn't known her scholastic struggles and peppered her with college and career questions. *They have online classes, you know. Isn't there anything you'd like to do?* She hadn't even told Ben how close she'd come to not graduating, and how often. Her desperation to stay on the gymnastics competitive team had fueled her manic drive to boost her grades. She and Austin had even studied together, his own struggles just as hard. Classmates thought chemistry drove them together time after time. And it had been. But not that kind. They'd once pulled an all-nighter studying molecular equations. She'd missed failing that test by one point.

Not everyone was cut out for college. Didn't mean she didn't have aspirations.

What would Travis's parents think of her? Mr. and Mrs. Walker had run a thriving farming business and raised three overachiever kids. If Travis brought her home, then what?

They have online courses, you know.

She hadn't revealed to any of Ben's family that she'd tried online courses. Between adjusting to a move and renting a house and new mom duties, she'd failed her first test in Accounting 101 and dropped the rest of the courses she had enrolled in. Ben had encouraged her to just stick with one course, he'd help her, but he'd been busy enough with his job that took him all over the county selling fertilizer. And he'd been working on his own associate degree.

She sighed. Waiting for Kambria sucked. Her in-laws liked to take their time, no matter how often Kami requested they get her home before her bedtime.

She tapped her fingers on the couch. Her stomach rumbled. Since it was her night off cooking, she'd only grabbed a sandwich.

A night off and she was going crazy by seven p.m.

Scrolling through her phone, she searched ranching forums and websites. Her dad had done this mostly by himself. She had to do it smarter. Be less impulsive and reactionary. She might have to keep one of her jobs, but ranching would still allow quality time with Kambria. Living in the country would give her daughter space to roam instead of sitting in the cramped apartment, watching TV until she got home. Kambria could have cats and dogs, maybe even a goat or two. She could join 4-H and show off her work at county fairs.

Kami tossed her phone aside as soon as she heard voices. She jumped up and threw open the door.

Kambria trudged past her. "Ugh, Mom. I'm so tired. Don't wake me up tomorrow; I want to finally sleep in." She disappeared into her room.

Kami turned a raised brow on Ben's dad.

Lee chuckled. "She's worked so hard all week, no wonder she's exhausted."

"Maybe if she'd gotten home earlier, she could've told me about it."

Lee brushed her off, either ignoring her or oblivious to her pointed tone. "Martha wanted to take her out for supper as a reward for working so hard. Well, I'll come pick her up Sunday. Listen, the academy starts early in the morning, so I'd better get her back to Normandy by five o'clock. See you at four then?"

Less than forty-eight hours with her daughter? She forced a smile. "She'll be excited, I'm sure."

"Yeah, we're loving it. Thanks for doing this." Lee left.

As if she had a choice. She went to Kambria's room and knocked lightly.

No answer. She cracked the door. Her little girl had crawled into bed fully clothed and was fast asleep.

She shut the door and stared at it.

So that was it. The night she looked forward to catching up with Kambria was over by eight. Never started in fact.

Fucking Martha and her selfish ways.

She stomped to her phone and opened her messages.

I have time tonight if you want to come over.

She sunk onto the couch and stared at the wall. Was he going to reply?

Her phone pinged.

Be there in twenty.

Travis was coming. She grinned and jumped up to change

out of her work outfit. She smelled like grease and coffee. Slipping into a solid T-shirt and leggings, she eyed herself in the mirror. Not exactly pajamas, but with easier access than jeans.

What was she thinking?

She didn't want to know. Darting into the bathroom, she dug out her brush and Kambria's detangler spray. It'd take the *eau de diner* out of her locks.

Her stomach growled again.

Travis was always ready for food. She scurried to the kitchen and looked through her cupboards and fridge. Nothing. She dug around her freezer and found ice cream. Dammit, what flavor was his favorite?

By the time she'd dished up two bowls, there was a knock on the door.

She opened it with a quiet, "Come in."

He stepped inside, his grin full of promise and his arms full of laptop.

Part of her appreciated that he came to work and hoped for more instead of thinking she was a sure thing.

"What happened to Kambria? Did she stay with your in-laws?"

Kami tipped her head to the hallway. "She went straight to her room after uttering a whole sentence. She's passed out."

"Ah." He settled on her sofa and turned on his computer. He kicked out his long legs in front of him. His boots were almost spotless. Had he worn his good pair for her? His shirt was impeccable even though he'd probably been in the field all day.

He'd dressed up and she'd dressed down.

But his gaze flicked to her leggings and licked the length of her legs. That's right. He'd never seen her out of her country girl wear. As a kid, she hadn't been out of jeans and boots unless she was in a leotard for a practice or a show.

He'd seen her out of her jeans, too.

Before the flush crept up to her cheeks, she went after their ice cream.

"What flavor did you like again?" She handed him the bowl.

He pried his eyes off the screen and glanced at the dish. "My favorite flavor is cold. Thanks."

She sat next to him, her leg propped between them like a wall of protection. Doing anything with him here was a bad idea, but if he started something, she didn't know if she could quit.

"You can't claim to be deprived of ice cream. There's no cooking."

"Yeah, but I never think of buying it."

She snorted. "Have a ten-year-old kid. They'll never let you forget."

He chuckled and clicked through his computer. His laughter had been genuine; she liked that about him. She'd didn't get the sense that he was humoring her, or trying to stay on her good side by tolerating Kambria.

That'd been a concern of hers when she'd decided to enter the dating pool again, and seeing Austin hadn't helped. She shouldn't care, but being alone sucked. Having a kid was the most wonderful thing in the world, but it could also be very isolating. Women her age had kids who were either younger, or it was like they feared her around their spouses.

And, well, she had history with a few of them, but it didn't mean she was "that girl" or that she'd ever been. No matter what people had said about her, they could never claim she was the other woman.

She'd done something right then, and now.

"Here's what I have." Travis rotated the computer so she

could see the screen. A neat, organized spreadsheet was open. "It's really not that bad. I think you might need to spray the pastures. Leafy spurge is prominent in all of your quarters, but that's not all bad news. The thistle is, though."

She opened her mouth to spill what was on her mind, but closed it.

He looked at her expectantly. When she didn't say anything, he asked, "Were you going to say something?"

"I've read some studies on training cattle to eat leafy spurge, or to use multi-species grazing, like sheep and I thought 'What about sheep?'"

He blinked. "Like ranching sheep?"

"Yeah. A smaller animal might be a little easier for me and they aren't as picky about their pastures. When I was in 4-H, I went to the McKenzies' farm, you know, on the other end of town, and her dad showed us how to shear. I've done some reading…"

Look who she was talking to. Travis was more well-read than her and probably knew everything out there. Or she was full of shit and he'd tell her so.

His eyes lit up. "There are some amazing possibilities in sheep. And I think you'd find sheep solve a lot of the problems you're facing with cattle."

"Like what?" She knew from her research, but she wanted to hear his take, since he was not only open to the idea, but excited.

He set his empty bowl down and twisted toward her, one hand steadying the computer. "They're easier to handle, for one. You can push and shove a sheep where you want it to go instead of getting a horse saddled to maneuver a cow to the barn. Sheep'll eat anything, even thistle."

She jumped in with her own findings. They traded information on annual income per sheep, diet needs, equipment needs. Travis sounded more thrilled than she was when she first stumbled across the article that planted the idea. He shut his laptop and rested it on the floor. She finished her treat and set the bowl down. Within minutes, they were facing each other, spouting wool facts.

"You seem fascinated by the subject." She laid her hand on his knee. Never in her life had she imagined sitting next to him discussing business. He hadn't brushed off anything she said, but expounded on it. He'd even asked for her business plan and when she blinked and nearly panicked that she'd make a fool of herself, he clarified by asking what her income ideas were regarding selling meat, wool, or milk.

Oh, that. She'd been forming a loose business plan the last few weeks. To be fair, she'd only had a couple of weeks to research and come up with a bare outline. Her gymnastics academy outline involved several documents and hours of research. And they were destined to sit in a folder on her computer.

Perhaps years after she was deep into mutton, she'd look back on all those files and snort at how inadequate they were for what it really took to run a business. By then, the longing in her heart should've died down.

They went over all the options and since nothing was set in stone, she found pure enjoyment in the conversation. Not so much about the details, but the back and forth between her and Travis.

At work, she didn't discuss what she was doing with her mom's land. Her coworkers were lovely and always inquired about Kambria. They'd trade kid or grandkid stories and commiserate about the job. She was afraid to discuss her ideas with her mom. The woman defaulted to her dad's old ways of raining on her parade. *How do you think you're going to do that? Can you really pull that hair-brained idea off?* If Dad was still around, she could hear him say *Why would you bring sheep to cattle country?*

Dad wasn't around. She brought her attention back to Travis mid-sentence.

"—and Cash said 'I ain't no wool wrangler' so I dropped it."

She smiled. Someone as smart as Travis got shot down, too?

She must've been staring at him, contemplating her newfound insight. He grew quiet, his expression serious. He drifted closer. She met him in the middle until their lips touched.

KAMI'S MOUTH was chilled from her cool treat, but her body was as hot as a late July afternoon. Travis gently pressed her back until they were stretched across her couch and he was cradled between her legs.

Her legs. Still muscular and curvy from her years in gymnastics, every single inch was on display in those leggings. He loved the roll of her hips in her jeans, the way the light danced off the glitter and sequins decorating her pockets. When she'd been performing, he'd sit in awe of her sheer talent that had been shaped by hard work. She'd been a spectacular athlete, all focus and determination. It was obvious the younger gymnasts looked up to her. He'd been all admiration then, and he was now.

She'd made a brilliant decision that would be pivotal in her success of acquiring her mom's property. Pam might be thrown for a loop, but it'd soon be clear that Kami knew what she was talking about.

A small whimper escaped her. Travis put most of the pressure on his knees to keep from crushing her and to keep his erection from grinding into her. She'd asked him over for help, not for sex. He'd let her decide whether he stayed or left.

She greedily deepened the kiss. It'd only been a day since they'd gotten each other off, but it'd been a long damn day. How many times had he spaced out because he was lost in remembering how she'd fallen apart in his arms. He'd shattered, and all she'd needed to use was one hand.

When her legs wrapped around his waist and she rocked into him, he lost himself in her. She wanted him, and he'd take whatever she gifted him with.

Already, his shaft throbbed. His body forgot all restraint around her. The orgasm she'd given him was stronger than any he'd experienced. What would it be like to climax inside of her? To lose himself in her wet heat as a grown man and not a boy who didn't really know what he was doing.

They thrust against each other harder, faster.

She broke the kiss, her hands on each side of his face. "If we do this, we need to go to the bedroom."

Words from heaven.

He pushed off her and held out his hand to help her up. She turned with a wicked gleam in her eye and led him to her bedroom. When he was all the way inside, she shut the door. The darkness of her room made it hard to make out more than a bed and some dressers, but he detected her simple no-nonsense style in here as in the rest of the place. He liked that about her. The sound of the lock being turned echoed among their breaths.

There were a few more considerations to doing this when there was a kid around.

"What if she wakes up?" he asked, keeping his voice low.

"Then we'll have to be quiet."

He yanked her to him. "I can do that."

Another searing kiss, but it only lasted a moment. They

were each in too much of a hurry. She drew her top over her head. He was mid-unbutton of his shirt, but stopped.

Whoa.

Spectacular breasts spilled out of a simple white, lace bra. She shimmied out of her bottoms and snapped the bra off.

Whoa.

Kami Lee Preston was naked.

"You're stunning." He lifted a lock of hair off her shoulder and brushed it back. Her ripened-wheat hair gave her skin an angelic glow, skin he'd feared he'd never see or touch again.

"You're fully dressed," she said.

He couldn't take his eyes off her as she finished undoing his shirt and shoved it down his arms. She started on his jeans next.

"Uh…" She dropped a kiss on his chest. He hadn't noticed he was holding his breath. "I need your help to get your pants off. Your boots are still on."

That spurred him into action. He toed off his boots and shucked his pants until he was as naked as her, erection straining for her.

She danced her fingers along his pectorals. "I can't believe a computer nerd like you has a body like this."

"Genetics. All the men in my family have the same body type."

She laughed softly. "This isn't science. It's hard work."

"Same with you." *Smooth, Walker.* He failed at romancing Kami Preston.

"Hard work has never been the problem with me."

Her words held an undercurrent of something deeper. Was it the lack of confidence? He had no idea how to make her see her own worth, but he could show her how much he thought of her.

He crooked a finger under her chin and tilted her face to look at him. Their gazes met for a second, electricity crackling between them until he closed the distance and claimed her mouth again.

He lowered his hand until he cupped a breast. Rolling her nipple between his fingers earned him a low moan.

Enough of this. He had to worship her properly.

Sweeping her off her feet, keeping the kiss in place so he swallowed her squeal of surprise.

He placed her on the bed, spreading himself over her. Kneeing her legs open, he wanted to do so much: taste her, ravish her, kiss every inch of her body. But he couldn't do that while his cock throbbed painfully. More than physical release, he wanted a connection with her, something between them that wasn't just about getting off.

And shit, his pants were on the floor behind him.

"I don't want to leave you," he whispered against her lips. "Do you have a condom close by?"

Nibbling a path to his ear, she simultaneously reached to her bed stand. Her fingers fell a few inches short.

He could barely think with her sharp teeth nipping his tender earlobe. If it was possible to grow even harder, he did.

He tugged her drawer open and snagged a packet. They weren't meant to be torn open with teeth, but that's what he did.

She released his ear to steal it from him and roll it on. Her touch on his cock almost jackknifed him off the bed. He lost all clear thought as she placed him at her entrance and tilted her hips up.

She hissed with pleasure. "I feel like we've been dancing around this forever."

"We have, each day an eternity."

Caressing his face, she gazed into his eyes as he thrust forward.

Oh god, this was nothing like he remembered.

So much better.

They weren't cramped in a car, worried they'd get busted. He wasn't terrified he'd ejaculate before he pleased her, or even entered her. She was his for the night, for as long as they could be quiet.

"Oh, Travis." Her tight heat clamped around his shaft, every quiver and twitch amping up his senses. He braced his arms on either side of her and took a few slow, intent thrusts.

She drew her knees up, the urgency as apparent in her face as the rest of her body. A low groan of satisfaction eased out of him. She craved this as badly as he did.

He changed the angle of his movements, monitoring her reactions before he settled on a steady rhythm that made it increasingly difficult for her to keep her volume down.

Her hands were all over him. On his shoulders. At his hips to coax a faster pace he refused to submit to. Fisting the comforter at her side. She rocked and moaned and bit her lip.

It was time. Watching her was enough to set off an orgasm, but to do it while her sex gripped his cock like a vice and she made those delicious sounds? Impossible.

Dropping to one elbow, he threaded a hand between them and found her clit. He didn't have to move his fingers; they were bouncing off each other enough, that was all the sensation her bundle of nerves needed.

She was growing louder, alternating biting her lip and gasping. Smashing their mouths together, he needed her as much as she needed him to damper their calls of passion.

Heat saturated his hand as she came—hard. His thrusts shortened out of necessity as he lowered his defenses and let the ecstasy flood him. She tightened around him, rode her climax, her legs like a vice, her sex gripping harder than her fist last night. Groaning into her, he shook through his release; if the room wasn't already black, his vision would've winked out. Managing to hold the worst of his weight off her, his arm was pinned between them; he prided himself on being with it enough to think of her needs.

They caught their breath together. He eased them to the side, missing the clasp of her body. His cock probably steamed in the cool air of the room.

"Think we were quiet enough?" he murmured.

She giggled and snuggled into him. "I wasn't paying attention. I hope so."

They were cuddling. He had Kami in his arms, reveling in their post-coital afterglow. His fantasy had played out, only now he knew it wasn't his real fantasy. One time experiencing this would never be enough.

CHAPTER 9

$\mathcal{K}$ ami hitched her breath, the swivel of her hips involuntary. Her gaze kept wanting to drift to the clock, the responsible adult in her hard to shut off.

It was after midnight and she was on top of Travis in the most provocative way she'd ever been with anyone.

Adult sex with Travis Walker was more mind-blowing than she'd imagined. He had the stamina of a man, the determination of someone who conquered anything he put his mind to, and the zeal of a guy who had limited time to fuck her.

Her knees quivered from bearing her weight. She clutched the headboard and glanced down. His tongue was as wicked and sharp as his mind, and it was driving her out of her mind. She'd called out too loudly so many times, she should phone Martha and thank her for wearing Kambria out.

Because sitting on Travis's face as he coerced another orgasm out of her was an unimaginable treat. She wanted to glance over her shoulder, see if he was stroking himself, or just ogle his erection. His cock was as fun to look at as the rest of his body. Thick and long, it had a mind of its own.

They'd only used one condom, but he had another ready on the pillow next to her knee.

He paused long enough to say, "You're going to stay right there, and after I taste you, I'm going to take you hard from behind. Don't let go of the headboard."

His rough voice against her sex was too much. When he wedged one finger inside of her, her orgasm hit hard.

"Travis! How am I—" She lost her question to a muffled shriek. How was she going to keep quiet?

Oh god. She was going to scream his name. Alternating cramming her lips closed and opening them to pant, she made it to the other end of her climax.

Sagging against the headboard, she rested her head against the wall. Could her neighbors hear her? She didn't really know them, and sex in her bedroom wasn't a common occurrence, but she'd never been pleasured like this.

He was careful when he slid out from under her. As she was about to twist around to collapse on the sheets, strong hands secured her waist. He released her only to don the condom, then he was pressing into her.

She didn't believe in comparing bed partners. Her only goal was to feel good at something, feel close to someone. But Travis filled her more completely than any other, both physically and metaphorically.

The knowledge staggered her. Her marriage to Ben had been far from empty. Her relationship with Austin was based on a mutual satisfaction that had disappointed her at first. He wanted more from her, but wasn't willing to give of himself. The lack of a selfish streak was what had attracted her to Ben after she gave up on her and Travis before they even started.

Her mind crashed into the present when Travis started to move. Her tender sex was willing to receive him, even open to another orgasm, though she had no idea how that was possible.

His big body surrounded her, one hand planted on the wall, the other digging into her hips. His hips swung, and she arched her back to stay open to him.

He dipped his head to whisper in her ear. Delicious shivers traveled up and down her spine.

"I can't believe how wonderful you feel. I love watching you come apart." Cool air drifted between them as he leaned back slightly. "I love watching us together, how your body receives me."

A shudder ran through her, his words affecting her as much as his actions. His pace increased; he must be close.

He grunted, his hand tightening to hold her still. His thrusts gained in force and speed. She might just orgasm with him.

"You have no idea how long I've dreamed of this, how much I've wanted you."

She blew out a breath, ready to submit to the sensations rolling through her, but she stared at the wall. Her pleasure plateaued.

Like… How long? Days? Years? Because that would be disturbing.

Were his words empty? A way to dull the pain, to take his mind off his lost love?

Kami didn't want to be the rebound girl. She wanted this to be real, not going through the motions, saying whatever sounded good during sex.

Were his emotions real or not? And who were they for?

Travis came, groaning his release, hugging her close to his chest. The bed bounced and squeaked with the movement. She wished she could enjoy cresting with him.

Was he thinking of her? Or wishing he were still with his fiancée?

Stupid. Stupid. She should've been thinking of all that since the first time he kissed her. Of all people, she knew what it was like to miss someone so badly, feeling like her destiny was to be alone.

When she'd been with Austin the first time since Ben's death, it'd been weird, disturbing. She feigned an orgasm and cried after she left Austin's place. Dating him might've even been to assuage the guilt that she'd slept with someone she didn't care deeply about. A way to make it feel like the sex meant something. Because that was what she wanted now. For lovemaking to be *part* of the relationship, not the *entire* relationship.

The heavy weight of his head rested on her shoulder. At some point, his arms had wrapped around her.

"I feel like I lost you." He lifted his head and brushed her hair out of her face, continuing the caress down her shoulder. "Are you all right?"

"It's just…a lot of sex." She was so glad he was behind her and that it was dark. Lying had never been her strength.

He abruptly pulled away and helped her settle between the sheets. Always the gentleman. Always considerate. Was she wrong to doubt this thing between them?

He stretched out next to her, but on top of the sheet. "I'm afraid I'll fall asleep if I stop moving." Shadows fell across his face, her digital clock the only source of light in the room. She could imagine his lopsided grin when he confessed that he was tired. Another quality that hooked her. A man like him could swagger around with no apologies, but he was always considerate.

"Are you sure everything's okay?"

Why couldn't he be oblivious to her emotional needs? "I'm fine. It's just…" Words piled up. If she opened her mouth, it all would come out. Her doubts about them weren't the thing on her mind. Would it hurt to share some of her concerns? "This, you and I, wasn't expected. I don't want people talking about me to Kambria the way they did to me about my mom."

He propped himself up on an elbow.

Before he could say anything, she rushed on. "I know what they all thought of me in high school." And they were right. She'd dated a lot of boys. She'd kissed a lot of boys. She'd had sex with more than a few boys. Her daughter shouldn't pay for decisions she'd made as a kid. "I don't want to do anything to get them talking again."

"You've been dating Austin." He'd said it measured, almost cautiously. "And you think if you're seen with me, it'll reignite the gossip mill."

"I felt like dating Austin put the speculation on simmer. If you and I go out in public, it might boil over. I don't trust how much people have grown up." She didn't want to trust and then get blindsided like she had when she'd been getting her hair done for prom and two ladies were commenting on how many men her mom had moved on with since Dad had died. The conversation was likely for Kami's benefit.

One of them had been Travis's mom.

"Are you still seeing him?"

"*No.* I'm here with you."

A crooked grin formed. "So, you're seeing me then?"

Oh. Um…

Tension thickened between them. She hadn't meant to hurt his feelings.

"I don't sleep around," she finally said. "But if people see me with you— I'm not ready to deal with that. And then there's your parents."

Shadows didn't mask his look of confusion. "What do they have to do with us?"

"I am one hundred percent certain that your mom won't approve of me." The defensive tightening of his shoulders was clear in the dark. "I overheard her slamming my mom's return to dating."

His groan brimmed with frustration and disappointment. "I'm so sorry."

"You don't need to apologize for her, but I already have one Martha in my life. I don't want to take on another during such a huge life transition."

"I'm still sorry you had to experience that. Mom can be… Mom." He paused, his finger caressing her cheek. "May I ask you something? Dillon and Elle are getting married. Will you accompany me? It's a few weeks away and we can make our debut then. If, you know, you still want to see me when the day rolls around."

His question was significant. He was asking her out in a major way, to announce they were a couple in a big way. This was what she'd just been questioning. Did he really want a serious relationship? Bringing her to his cousin who was like a brother's wedding made a bold statement.

"I don't know." The whole mom deal would be out there, too.

"I understand." He sounded crestfallen. Panic bloomed in her chest.

"I don't want to quit seeing you." She paused to collect her thoughts. Ultimately, it wasn't about her. "I have to do what's best for Kambria. I won't be able to give you an answer until closer to the date." A family wedding! She'd have to grow a giant pair of lady balls before she strode into the chapel on his arm. The mischievous voice in her head said she should get a sweater made with "STU" stamped on it. "Maybe you should ask someone else so they can plan the number of guests."

"I'm not going with anyone else," he said quietly. A plain statement. He rolled close enough to kiss her, a quick but firm peck on the lips. "You think about it. I'm in the field tomorrow, but I'll saddle up Mandrell and ride out on Reba to check on you. Kambria can go for another spin. Mandrell won't mind."

As he got out of bed and dressed, she dug through a drawer until she found a nightshirt and shorts. He finished dressing, and she peeked out to make sure Kambria hadn't woken.

They tiptoed to the front door, his hand on the small of her back. Lifting her chin, he gave her one last lingering kiss.

The door shut behind him. Crossing her fingers, she hoped her neighbors weren't awake and spreading the news that Travis Walker was leaving her place at one in the morning.

She turned her back and slumped against the door, staring down the hall at her bedroom. Going back to a bed where she'd be surrounded by his masculine scent was a special torture. How nice would it have been to wake up in his arms?

She was confident it would've been heaven, but her daughter came first. Any drama between her and Travis would spill over onto Kambria.

TRAVIS GROANED and rolled to his side. Between the vibrating phone on the nightstand and the pounding on his front door, he couldn't cover his head and snatch a couple more hours of sleep.

Shoving off the mattress, he snagged his phone. He shuffled to the front door as he checked the screen.

Four missed calls. One from an hour ago and three in the last two minutes, all from Aaron.

He blinked and peered at the numbers. It was after ten in the morning?

The pounding on the door didn't cease. Fatigue peeled away from him. Fully awake, he opened the door to an irate Aaron, phone to his ear, fist poised for another knock.

"Dude." Aaron clicked his phone off, concern draining out of his deep blue eyes. "Did you tie one on last night? I've been waiting for you for a couple of hours."

"Dammit, I'm sorry. I didn't get to bed until late last night." After reliving the most erotic night of his life, sleep had been a hard beast to tame. "I'll get dressed and grab my stuff."

He let the door swing open and turned away. Aaron entered, but didn't follow him to his room. "Why the late night?"

"Just couldn't sleep," Travis called over his shoulder. He rustled around for clean clothes and pulled on a pair of jeans and a green Under Armor shirt. The top was already ripped from getting snagged on the workbench in his shop. It'd probably find a couple more tears before he finally threw it away. He meandered back out to grab his boots and take a seat on the entry bench.

"Kami English keeping you awake?"

Travis paused pulling on his work boots. "Why would you say that? And it's Preston."

Aaron cocked a brown brow. "I was joking, but I think I touched on something."

"Don't go saying shit like that," he grumbled and finished stomping into his boot.

"Why not—if it's true?"

"It's not true." He couldn't look his cousin in the eye. He was a shit liar, always too open and honest, worried what they'd think if he was busted.

"Uh-huh. But if it were, why hide it?"

Travis finally looked up and glowered at Aaron. From his cousin's crooked hat and his rumpled clothes, down to his feet shoved into boots without a care to where his pant legs landed, it was easy to fall for the bait that Aaron wasn't keenly intelligent. He was always distracted with some problem, or with his family's several problems, that he rarely paid any attention to his appearance.

For a heartbeat, Travis envied him. Aaron never had girl trouble. They seemed attracted to him, but ran the other way once they sniffed a hint of his family drama. And Travis knew that bothered him. But to be saved from the upheaval Michelle had caused in his life before she died, Travis would rather she'd friend-zoned him long before they'd gotten serious. Now with Kami…two adults sneaking around? If it was just for her daughter, he'd understand, but he sensed another reason and it brought out the heartbroken kid who was stood up on a Friday night.

"People talk," he finally answered. "It wouldn't be fair to her if rumors were started."

Aaron chuffed. Catching his reflection in the mirror by the coat hooks, he adjusted his hat. "Hell, I know people talk. Believe me. It's usually not a good thing when they do. What's Kami worried about, though? She's a single woman, unless you count Austin hopping in and out of her bed."

Travis's glower turned into a scowl. Not anymore, dammit.

Aaron peered at him. "You lying son of a bitch. You and Kami have something going on?"

"No. Yes. No. Aaron, just stop." Travis buried his head in his hands. What a mess. He'd just had this discussion with Kami and now he was spilling their business to Aaron. He and Aaron were close in age, younger than Cash and Dillon but older than Brock, and were tight, best friends even. It didn't change that this felt like a betrayal to Kami. And to Aaron. What would he think of Travis dating so soon?

"You're seeing her, or you're not. I don't get why either one would be a big deal." Aaron crossed his arms.

"Other than the fact that she has a little girl and doesn't want to have the same reputation as Pam, there's Michelle."

"I can see that, all of it. But it's not like you and Kami are serious. Fuck what everyone else thinks."

Travis dropped his hands. Was that part of Kami's hesitation? That people would think he was using her to get over Michelle? Fifteen months had gone by agonizingly slow, yet it'd passed in a blink. He was ready to move on, but at the same time, he wanted to savor the chemistry between them. Before parents and in-laws and passersby added their two cents. After all, there was a ten-year-old girl to consider. That was something Aaron would understand.

"We don't want our business affecting her daughter, so can you please keep this to yourself?"

Aaron sobered. "Absolutely."

Travis rose, chose his dirty hat for a day in the field, and settled it on his head. "Mind if we take separate trucks? I've got plans this afternoon."

TRAVIS ADJUSTED Mandrell's lead rope. The sway of the horses chased off the worries that had plagued him all day. A warm breeze kept the mosquitoes away but had gained in strength. Thick, puffy clouds blocked the sun for long periods of time, cooling the day enough to call it chilly. Then the sun would peek out and infuse his body with heat.

A nearly perfect day to ride.

The day he'd taken Reba to snoop on Kami had also been his first time out for the year. Unless he was helping with the ranch, he rarely rode for pleasure. Times like this made him wonder why he wasn't out every day for a little equine therapy.

Because when he wasn't working, he was buried in his computer. His family thought the app he'd made was cool and constantly tossed out ideas of what he should do next. It was like his computer skills were an exotic talent, a point of awe for them. Sure, his cousins had their phones and their own laptops, but they only did what they needed to, spending the rest of their time working or socializing.

But he'd had Michelle, who was usually out of town, and once he mentioned his idea for a game, they'd been so thrilled, he'd had to develop it.

He should design another.

A cloud drifted in front of the sun, momentarily shading the pasture he rode through. Continuing on its path, the cloud floated on and the sun brightened the day.

His computer could wait. This was nice.

He rode through the pasture closest to his property. There were no signs of Kami. He reached the road that would take him to Pam's house. His house and hers weren't far apart, but no road ran between them. His family's pastures and a couple of the biggest fields they worked were in between. Pam's land spread out from there, but to get to her place, he'd have to take the next turn off the highway.

By horse was much better.

Steering Reba through the ditch, Mandrell followed. They turned to go down the drive to Pam's. A spindly form ran down the road to meet him.

"Travis!" She jumped and did a cartwheel, as graceful her mom at that age. More so, because she'd probably been taught by her mom. She slowed as she reached them. "Mom said you might be coming by with Mandrell today. Can I really ride?"

"After I talk to your mom."

"This way." She darted off.

Reba nickered. Travis patted her neck. "To have that energy again, am I right?"

When he reached the circular driveway, Kami strode out of the sagging red barn with Kambria. A flutter of apprehension had him readjusting in his seat. His gaze swept from her to the barn. The large barn door was open. How, he didn't know. The structure of the barn had altered so much from age and weather, the door should've been jammed closed.

The mustiness grew stronger as he approached. No lights were on inside, but he could make out piles of boxes amid old equipment.

Kami wiped an arm across her forehead, drawing his attention back. She murmured to Kambria, a smile lighting her face. She'd wrapped a bandanna around her forehead and was back in her frayed jeans and a snug, long-sleeved purple shirt. The sleeves were a good choice if she was digging around in the dump inside the barn.

Kami turned her grin his way. "Hey, you made it. And made a young girl very happy."

"I was thinking on my way here that I owe her a thanks. I don't know the last time I rode so much for fun instead of work."

"You ride for work?" The awe in Kambria's voice made him feel ten feet tall.

Too bad he wasn't, he could fix the roof of that barn—if there was any way to fix it. A match might be the best solution.

He swung down from Reba and handed her lead rope to Kami. Their gazes met. Her cheeks pinked and she glanced away. Yeah, he probably wasn't covering his thoughts about her well. All grimy and sweaty and he'd love nothing more than to ride off with her.

But she had work, and he had a promise to keep.

He went to give Kambria a boost, but she clambered onto Mandrell with little help.

He turned back to Kami. "I feel awful riding off while you're here working."

"Don't be. I won't have her asking me every ten minutes if it's time to go home or time for supper."

Kambria scrunched her nose. "Grandma doesn't have cable—or horses."

He jutted his chin toward the dilapidated barn. "Are you sure it's safe to work in there?"

"No. I figured if it didn't collapse when I opened the door I should be okay for a while. I uncovered an old tractor I bet I could get running again with a YouTube video and a prayer."

He chuckled but kept the barn in the corner of his eye. "Be careful."

"Always. You, too."

They sauntered off. Kambria didn't quit chatting the entire time, and he probably hadn't quit grinning. His brother and sister didn't make it home often, but Kambria reminded him of them when they were younger. None of them had kids, and neither did any of his cousins. He hadn't realized how boring it could get without them.

"You like my mom."

He glanced at Kambria, his brows lifted. There was no use lying. The girl was smart. "I do. We've known each other a long time."

"She's known Austin a long time and he's still a douche."

He snorted, tried to recover, but couldn't help his snicker. "I agree."

"I didn't like how he treated her."

"How's that?" Could a grown man be nosy?

"He's always, um…disagreeing? Dismissing? I dunno, but

he's, like, rude enough that it makes me mad. And he doesn't like me."

"Was he rude to you?" He sharpened his gaze on her. As if he needed any more reason to dislike that bastard.

She shrugged. "He ignores me. I know he used to call Mom when I was at Grandma and Grandpa's."

"And you didn't like that?"

"She can do better."

"I agree."

She shot him a small smile. Either she liked how much he agreed with her, or she liked him. Unless she just didn't see him as a contender for her mom's heart. They rode in silence for a few minutes before Kambria hit him with rapid-fire questions about horses and gear. The rest of the ride involved him spewing his knowledge of all things equine. After a couple of hours, he guided them back to Pam's. Sunset was a couple of hours away, but the temperature had dropped slightly.

Kami was sitting on the porch steps. Her smile when she saw Kambria was brighter than a clear summer day. When she turned it on Travis, he swallowed hard.

She rose and sauntered toward them. Kambria handed off her lead and slid down while gushing her thanks. She ran off before Travis could reply.

"Oh no," Kami said. "Is she getting out of caring for the horses and tack?"

"It's no problem. I know she'd do it if we were at my place."

"You probably wouldn't get her to stop brushing the horses."

He swung down, but kept an arm propped on the saddle. After his talk with Kambria, he was more conscious of being too forward with Kami. The girl picked up on a lot for seeming to be constantly distracted.

"I'd offer another ride for tomorrow, but I suppose she's going back to Normandy."

Irritation rippled over Kami's face. "Yep. They have it all planned." She smiled shyly up at him. "Do you want me to go back to the supper arrangement tomorrow night?"

Hell, yes. "If you want to save a starving man, it's the right thing to do. But I know you're busy here."

"I'll head to your place and start cooking after they pick her up."

No one was around, but he lowered his voice. "Should I come prepared for dessert?"

Her gaze darted to the house and back to him, a gleam of desire in the depths of her honey-brown eyes. "You better believe it."

She sashayed away, leaving him to figure out how to get back on Reba with a pounding erection.

CHAPTER 10

Kami eyed the crowd. Good lord. She was going to be deaf by the time she was forty if she kept picking up bartending shifts. The steady roar of the crowd was even worse tonight because it was the night of the bar's street dance. Even with a portion of the street roped off for the customers to spill out to, the bar was packed. The band would start soon, then bass would reverberate through the place. Her ears had rung for a full day after the last street dance she'd worked.

Ugh, she should've asked some questions when her coworker frantically called her to fill in. She'd had a family conflict and Kami had zero conflict because Kambria wasn't home this weekend. Waiting for Travis to call and invite her over since it wasn't her assigned night to cook smacked too much of desperation, and she'd picked up the shift. What had motivated her was the dread of the phone not ringing.

The entire week she'd ended up in his bed after they ate. As soon as dishes were loaded into the washer, he'd take her on the counter, on the table, on the floor—it didn't matter. The man was insatiable, and she'd thought she had a healthy sexual appetite. He was inventive, too. Just the night before, she hadn't even left her seat before he had her stripped down and had her legs over his shoulders.

She cut off that line of thinking before she blushed and made the typical handsy customers think she was open to getting hit on and groped.

Her manager draped a dishrag over his shoulder; she suspected because he thought it made him seem dapper and worldly as he flirted with all the single ladies. And Kyle had been doing this long enough that he knew who was single, who wasn't, and who was single for the night.

He lifted his chin to point to the door to the outdoor section. "Wanna help Megan out there? A big group just came in and she's swamped already."

She wove her way through the crowd, excited for some fresh air. Only an hour to go on her shift and she'd get to hear some good country music and enjoy the beautiful night.

"Oh, thank you Jesus." Megan grabbed her arm and pointed to the far end where a crowd had gathered around one of the long tables. "Like ten of them walked in. I'm dying here, and I wish I could serve them. The Walkers are always good to us."

Excitement escalated while her stomach plummeted. The Walkers? That many of them? Her gut changed direction and crawled into her throat.

Was Travis here? And if he was, what would he do when she waited on him? Would he dance with anyone? If he did, was it any of her business?

She counted the Walkers as she made her way over. Eight. Five men and three women.

Her palms were sweaty, and her heart rate kicked up. She'd rather face a hoard of annoyed badgers than pretend in front of Travis and his family that she hadn't had sex with him every night this week. What would they do if they found out about her? He'd be on the receiving end of well-meaning family lectures, and they'd all be right. Kami would be the first to agree that she wasn't good enough for him. But she wanted him more than anyone else. Did that count?

She forced a smile to her face and prayed it didn't look fake. At almost twenty-nine, she was too old for this shit. The death of a husband did that to a girl.

Five pairs of blue eyes that varied in shade landed on her as soon as she approached. The Walkers were the golden boys of the county. Good kids who'd never been in trouble with the law, who defended each other religiously, and played a mean game of whatever sport they were involved in. They'd all grown up to be respectable men who lent a hand wherever needed. Travis should despise her after the trouble her dad gave his family but both he and Cash had helped her. She should despise Travis for the way his parents treated hers, but couldn't. Those were problems for someone else; she had enough of her own.

"What can I get you?" Her voice didn't shake, which was quite a feat. She'd placed herself at the end of the table where Travis sat across from Aaron. As much as she wanted to avoid a potentially awkward situation, she was a damn adult.

Her mind clicked through the talk around town to identify the women. Three of the Walker Five were engaged, including Cash. The news had sheared through the bar, devastating many ladies, all with wistful well-wishes.

She'd been irritated and purposely ignored every one of those conversations. When she'd left town to marry Ben, all her mom had heard were outrageous inquiries and guffaws of how long it'd last.

The attractive woman smashed into Dillon's side spoke first. "We'll each have a root beer."

Brock's fiancée ordered for them both; Cash and his woman ordered separately. Aaron gave Kami a speculative look when he ordered, but overall, the rest of the table played it cool.

Finally, it was Travis's turn. "How's it going?"

Relief that he didn't "play it cool" mixed with a spike of anxiety that all attention would be on her.

And it was.

"Good. It's a busy night."

"You worked at your mom's all day before this?"

She nodded. "Trying to get that little John Deere running. I think it will with a new battery."

"Hey, Kami." Cash leaned over so he didn't have to shout. "Have you gotten anyone to hay your north pasture yet?"

"No, I was going to talk to..." She couldn't summon a name—because she hadn't gotten around to thinking about it yet. Cash pointed to himself, his eyes bright. "You?"

"Sure." He grinned. "I'd have to haul a load from across the county and Old Man Furness raised his rates."

"Call me with the details and we'll talk." She glanced back to Travis. Her heart waltzed into her throat at the gleam in his yes. "What are you drinking tonight?"

"Bud Light. Are you almost done working?"

She hesitated. The entire table was watching them.

"I have a little time left," she said. "But I think I might go home." And she would. This drama was killing her after a long day in the dust, tinkering with old engines that might never run again.

"You're welcome to hang out with us for a bit. I hear the band is great." The open invitation in his voice almost swayed her. They enjoyed conversation over dinner each night and every time her hopes rose. Could they really work?

Every morning, she'd wake up and talk sense into herself. Without Kambria home, the solitude rushed back with all the feelings of abandonment and loneliness after Ben's death. The crash back to reality was getting harder and harder, like the excitement of what could be forming with Travis amplified those emotions. Because if she had to go back to that state of mind, it'd be ten times worse.

"We'll see." Her resolve to head home wavered. A fun night out with other adults was tempting, but she didn't want to undo the reputation she was building. "I'll be back with your order."

Her last hour passed way too fast. The night was so busy that she only had time to check on the Walker's group once, but the burn of Travis's gaze followed her all over the outdoor seating area.

She clocked out with her manager and wistfully glanced toward the band. Their music filtered through the din of the bar and started her boot tapping. Gymnastics was tied closely to dance; it was natural for her to want to move to any beat she heard. Moore never had an official dance program, but she and the other cheerleaders infused their routines with rhythm.

All the Walkers were out on the dance floor, even Travis. They were stomping through a line dance. A smile played across her lips. The guy could move, on and off the dance floor. Had he and his fiancée been one of those couples that glided across the floor, completely in sync?

Bless Ben's heart, but he'd only been able to do the side-to-side shuffle. They'd had some good laughs over it, and he'd made up for the defect by being a superb father and an excellent partner.

She blinked back a sudden sting of tears. Finding both qualities in another man sometimes seemed impossible. Staying felt like she was handing Travis a lot of power over her heart.

The bass-thumping song ended, and a slower one started. Every Walker but Travis twirled a woman into their arms.

Travis meandered back to the table, looking around, probably for her.

She couldn't leave him hanging. Pushing her way back out to the street, she kept her eyes on him. All the single ladies he walked past eyed him with a spark of hope. She knew how they felt.

Large clusters of people blocked what should've been a straight path to Travis. She side-stepped one crowd when a young woman tugged on Travis's elbow. Kami stopped in her indecision to watch it play out or stomp over and claim her man.

Travis's smile was real and he gave the lady a huge hug.

Kami's feet were rooted. Stay or go? Dancing was either a fun activity between two partners or an intimate moment between a couple. She didn't know how Travis perceived it.

He slung his arms around the girl's shoulder, laughing, and strode to the dance floor.

Kami heart cracked. She spun as he happened to glance her way. He might've seen her, but she kept pushing through the crowd.

"Kami!" Travis reached her. Did the crowd part just for him when she'd had to elbow her way through? "Is everything okay?" His voice wasn't full of challenge, just concern aimed at her.

She couldn't decide which was worse. Her jealousy at seeing him with another woman, or that he'd made a small scene pursuing her.

TRAVIS HAD to give up ground to Kami's flight in order to follow her through the throng of people. Her shoulders were rigid and her chin high.

She pursed her lips like she was contemplating something to say, but settled on, "Fine." She continued her trek outside.

He followed her through the bar and out the exit. She didn't stop.

"Kami."

She looked over her shoulder, surprise etched across her face. "Why'd you follow me?"

"Because you look like you were upset. And I've been waiting to get you to myself all night."

"You seemed to be doing well." He detected anger, but a deeper emotion made him pause. Vulnerability. Surely not his Kami. She was the strongest woman he knew.

"That girl you saw me with was my cousin Bunny." He'd been itching to dance with Kami all night, hold her in his arms in front of everyone. His cousins were the only other women he'd dance with, except for his future cousins-in-law, besides Kami.

Her head tipped back and she sighed. "I'm so fucking stupid," she muttered.

"Why?" He waited. Had she been jealous? Jealous meant she cared—he hoped.

A couple blew out of the bar, the woman giggling into the man's neck. They looked like they were heading to do what Travis really wanted to do.

He turned his attention back to Kami. Exhaustion was etched over her face, and the source wasn't from just physical labor.

"Come on. Talk to me."

"I'm just having trouble with what I'm feeling right now and all I want to do is go home and work it out."

"Why not talk to me about it?"

"Because..." Her gaze tore from his to stare at the lot packed full of cars. "Because talking isn't what we usually do when we're together."

Where'd that come from? "Isn't it? I recall you asking me about our crops and what our company planted and why. And then there was the time you demanded I show you the game I designed. I know I love hearing updates about your daughter because your face brightens and you can't quit smiling when you talk about her. And don't get me started on sheep, because you and I can go for hours on that subject."

"Yeah, but that's all—"

"It's what people talk about when they enjoy each other's company."

She pursed her lips and met his gaze. "Doesn't it strike you as a little superficial?"

He planted his hands on his hips. The move might be aggressive, but if he didn't secure his hands, he'd grab her and kiss her in front of the few people coming and going from the bar. "You don't think we talk about our thoughts and feelings enough? Fine. Here's what I felt when I saw you. Desperate. Distraught at the sea of people between us. Usually, I spend most of my day watching the clock because all I want to do is go home and see you. Yeah, I like what we do together. Fuck, yeah. But I like just being with you."

She stared at him, her expression a mixture of stunned and...pleased?

"Now your turn," he said.

"What?"

"I don't know if you know this, but you don't talk about yourself much. I can tell you're holding out on me, and I don't know if it's me, or you."

"I do not hold back." She frowned.

He raised his brows. Yep. It was dawning on her that, no, she didn't. She scowled.

He broke into a grin. "Do you have your car?" She nodded. "I rode with Aaron, but they're all busy. Let's go somewhere and just talk. About real things." Her look was skeptical. He raised his hands in innocence. "I promise to do nothing other than give you a chaste good-night kiss."

The corner of her mouth hitched up. "I might hate you for your promise at the end of the night."

He wouldn't. It'd be worth it if she started trusting him.

She led him to her car. He folded himself inside.

She started the engine. "Why don't I just give you a ride home and we can have our little talk? I want to get to Mom's early tomorrow."

"What are you working on?"

"I'm going to get that riding lawn mower running even if it kills me."

He wished she hadn't found that thing; he wanted her day free. "Can you at least roll it out of the barn?"

"It won't budge, but I get enough light if I open the doors."

"It's not the light I'm worried about."

"It'll be fine. If Cash hays the pastures, that'll really help. I'm going to price fences. I think I'll rent the field, try my hand at sheep, and use the smaller pasture closest to the house for horses like Daddy did."

Her intentions were sound. "I know a family of five guys who farm and might like to rent your land."

She didn't look as thrilled as he hoped. "I feel like a charity case for you guys."

"Why?" He shook his head. "You misunderstand. Yes, my cousins lent a hand because I asked them to, but you're our neighbor. Hauling hay from your place is cheaper and easier. Renting those two quarters would also be cheaper and easier. If we could cut a road between my house and yours, it'd be cake." Taking the tractor and combine the long way was still a better option if they couldn't outright buy the space. "And we aren't our parents," he said quietly.

She cast him a sidelong look before bringing her attention back to the road.

He rallied himself for what he really wanted to ask. The question that had flagged him for over a decade.

"Why'd you sleep with me and then never talk to me again that summer?"

There. That was no superficial question.

"Wow. You're going right there. I guess I asked for it." She sure did. "I really liked you and everything that happened that night. But I told Austin I was meeting with you later when he asked me out and he pointed out that you and I didn't have anything in common."

"We have a shit-ton in common, and that's a technical term."

"Other than growing up around each other? You played football, I cheered for football. We rode horses. That's about it. School wasn't hard for you. When I heard you talking with your friends, it wasn't about fantasy football or the best cleats for the game. You guys argued about GMOs and whether organic farming really could be organic and on what scale would it be sustainable."

"And? You were obviously listening in. I doubt it was because it bored you."

A pinch formed between her brows. He watched her emotions play across her face. She hadn't connected the two. She hadn't paid attention just to prove that she wasn't good enough for him.

"I had nothing going for me. I barely graduated. I wasn't going to college."

"But you graduated. And you could go to college. I refuse to believe any excuse you give. The girl who barrel raced and did flips in the air could do anything she put her mind to."

She threw a hand up, keeping her other on the wheel.

"Don't you see? It's all physical. I never said I wasn't a hard worker."

"Why'd you marry Ben?" Her mouth dropped open. Hell, he'd surprised himself with the question. "You don't do anything without reason. You never have. I know it wasn't because of Kambria."

"Ben treated everyone the same, with respect and compassion. All he wanted out of life was to live and work and spend time with the people he loved." A tear rolled down her cheek. He brushed it away. He thought she'd quit, but she kept going. "I haven't told anyone, but I tried to take online classes. I failed. He didn't ridicule me, though." She sniffed. "Austin would've. Mom would've said 'I told you so' without really saying the words. So I didn't go to college? He didn't care. Was I happy? That was all he cared about. If he worked at the same job for forty years and we never moved from Normandy, he wouldn't have cared. I liked that about him. We were happy being mediocre."

Tears rolled too fast for him to keep up. "That sounds way more than mediocre, Kami."

She rubbed her face. "You're right. It was."

When she said that, he and Ben were the same guy. His parents had a hard time understanding why he wanted to come back and farm. He'd pursued an agriculture degree in hopes they'd realized his passion was the land. The science behind farming, the giant game of chance every farmer took each year.

"I was born in my house. Did you know that?"

She sniffled again and shook her head. She turned down the road that led to his place.

He nodded. "Mom didn't think it'd go so fast. No one did. So she thought she'd play it cool, not be the first-time mom who panics over all the details. But she waited too long. They called the ambulance, but Dad delivered me. My bedroom now is the same one I was born in."

"That's really cool." Said like she didn't know why he was telling her after she spilled her heart about her husband.

"Yeah. I'm tied to the place. Moore is my home. If I never move, I'm okay." He almost said he hadn't wanted to go to school. It was expected of him. But he couldn't bring himself to. He trusted Kami, but if he let the floodgates down and mentioned it around his parents, they'd be so disappointed. All the couples in their fifty-five-plus housing knew about his degrees. They all played his game. His parents gave him regular updates.

"What are you trying to say?"

"I'm just a guy, Kami."

"You're not like other guys. You can't see it, and that speaks a lot about your character. Your family is not like other families."

He was losing ground. "We have our problems."

She pulled in to his yard and parked in her normal spot. "Does the whole town know about them?"

He was about to say "probably" but he paused. Dillon's drinking problem had been deeply personal and he'd hidden it well. Brock had finally told the rest of them about his autism diagnosis, but they were all highly protective of him, and if he didn't tell anyone else, neither would they. Cash was the exception. It was common knowledge that he'd been a playboy and the older generation remembered that he wasn't his mom's biological child, but the product of an affair. Aaron's parents had moved back in with him in a case of reverse empty nest, but that was hardly the talk of the town.

Kami's dad, on the other hand... He'd blustered through town, leaving a wake of whispered conversations. *Inept. Moronic. That poor wife of his.* The only time he'd heard anything other than derision aimed at Pam English. Travis remembered the day clearly when Earl English passed away and left Pam a single mom. Mom and Dad had whispered their own conversations and speculations about why and what would happen to his wife and daughter.

Yet, no one reached out to help them. He'd asked his parents one day if they were going to. His dad had shrugged and said maybe. That was as far as it went. To be fair, Pam would've bitten a few fingers off. She wasn't as tyrannical as Earl, but just as atrocious at asking for help.

"Okay, I'll give you that one," he said.

She broke into a smile. "This talking feelings kind of sucks."

"I disagree. I've learned a lot. Now, my next question is where do we go from here?"

"Well, you ditched Bunny to chase after me, so I don't know how much longer we can keep it between us."

"Between us and all my cousins." When her eyes widened, he chuckled. "It's the curse of growing up so close. They can read me well."

She traced the steering wheel and looked out the windshield. The car was running, the AC at a comfortable level. They could talk all night. "I guess I can RSVP as your plus one to Dillon's wedding."

Best news ever. "Great. And before then?"

"This week will be the same as last week." She glanced at him through her lashes. His blood heated and pooled south. No touching. No touching. He would not go back on his word. "Then Kambria's back home this weekend. Then another week," another hesitant smile, "and the wedding. Unless you want to debut earlier."

"I want you to myself," he growled.

"Then we're agreed." She nodded once and stared back out the window.

"What's going on in that dynamic little head of yours?"

Her mouth quirked, but she didn't answer right away. Was he going to get a response? The longer she waited, the less sure he was. Finally, she spoke. "It's after the wedding I'm worried about."

He didn't speak. She was smart enough to know that he'd want an explanation.

"We're not our parents, but we still have to face our parents. I don't think my mom has anything more than general animosity toward you, but you've been so generous with your time." She shot him a wry grin. "And, of course, Kambria has filled her in on how great you are."

An unexpected boon of giving lessons. "I'm an adult, and I want to date you. I've wanted to date you for years. Mom and Dad will just have to deal."

She gave him a questioning look. "You've said that before. But there's over eleven years and an entire relationship in there for you."

His humor died, and he thought quickly. "I'm not talking about those years. When you ran into me at the bar that night, it was like no time had passed. I've had a terrible crush on you since I first saw you, Kami Lee Preston."

How could he show her that this was as real as it gets? That his infatuation with her preceded him and Michelle, her and Ben—her and anyone. It was always her. He'd wanted to live in his house, farm his land, and marry his woman. For years, all he'd had was his house. The years he tolerated school were bearable because he knew he was going back home. All those extra years for graduate school was all in the name of the farm, so they could pass strong and healthy land down to their children. Michelle had been his woman, but she hadn't. She'd wanted nothing to do with Moore or his farm. If it wasn't cutting edge ag research, her interest plummeted.

He couldn't touch Kami and communicate with his body that she was all he'd ever wanted. He couldn't tell her that he was about to dump his fiancée as she was breathing her last breath. How could he show Kami how much she meant to him?

A memory rippled to the surface. "Remember the first day of kindergarten when we got on the bus?"

She thought for a moment. "You and your cousins were the last ones picked up and there were no seats left?"

He nodded. "The middle schoolers were taking up all the room. Dillon and Cash found a seat, I gave Brock the spot by Aaron, and I was left in the middle of the aisle holding up the bus. Then you yelled 'Move your butts. Can't you see the guy needs a seat?'"

She gasped, covering her mouth. "I totally remember that. I was such a mouthy kid."

"You made quite an impression on me. I was dismayed to find out your dad was 'that neighbor,' but you captured my complete attention that day."

"My dad…" Her smile fell. "It's no mystery who I emulated."

Travis snorted, and she looked offended for a heartbeat until he clarified. "You don't think your mom had anything to do with that?"

Understanding lightened her gaze. "Yes, but not then, not around Dad."

"Serious?"

Dipping her head, she had an almost apologetic look. "She didn't talk back to Dad. I dunno. He was so much older than her, and I think she saw him as an authority figure. I know I did."

"You miss him, too?"

"Of course, but not like Ben. Dad wasn't healthy. You only had to spend five minutes with him to know his blood pressure was hammering at his heart. He ate antacids like breath mints." Her expression turned melancholy. "His death was easier to accept."

Much of their night was spent discussing death. He might as well push his point about her insecurities. "Michelle's death is hard to accept. She was, essentially, one of my best friends. But I've been surrounded by family ever since and it's made it easier to accept."

That was the best he could explain it without confessing the twist that made the situation even more tragic than it was.

"I'm sorry I stood you up that night, when we were supposed to meet for a movie. I almost ignored Austin, but I had gymnastics practice and the girls, you know"—she sighed—"asked about you. I could hear it in their voices. The disbelief."

"Give me a chance. I don't care about proving anyone wrong, I want to prove myself right."

Their gazes met and held, his breath suspended. She grasped his hand and gave it a squeeze. "I want you to, too. I guess this is it until Monday night. Homemade pizza night?"

"You know I eat whatever you make." He leaned in close, his breath tickling her ear. "And I have some ideas that involve you and the back-porch swing."

Her inhale was audible, and he grinned. An hour ago, he feared the worst. But here he was with his house, his farm, and his woman.

CHAPTER 11

Travis wrapped up chores with his cousins. All five of them had pitched in to help Cash get the cows fed. The wedding was slated for early afternoon and they all needed to shower and don their church clothes. Aaron and Brock had taken off already, but Travis hung back. His parents would probably be at the house by the time he got back, maybe even his brother and sister.

His whole family would be together. Shouldn't he be excited? The last time both his siblings had come home was for Michelle's funeral.

"Ready, man?" Cash had his arms propped on the side of the pickup. Abbi was inside, and Cash's furtive glances to the house made Travis think he wanted to join her in the shower.

Dillon adjusted his hat and stared across the yard, his expression contemplative. "More than ready. I knew Elle was it when I first saw her." He switched his gaze to Travis. "You're ready for your big date?"

Travis ducked his head. "Will it be a conflict that our big reveal is at the church?"

Dillon's serious expression didn't change. "If anyone gives you a hard time about it, have them talk to me."

Travis let out a slow breath of relief, but his concern didn't dissolve. "This day is your day, Dillon. I don't want it to be about me. Kami and I will deal with any issues that come up. These last few weeks with her—" Travis tried not recall her sprawled on his floor with him prowling up her body, "—have been really good. I'm in a good place, and I just want it to keep improving. We can't do that in secret."

He'd gone home after work. Kami had been there. They'd talked and laughed, had sex. These last few weeks were a dream come true, and he'd had to keep it all to himself.

Until he had to talk to his family. He hadn't told either Mom or Dad about his budding relationship. He'd mentioned he had a date, that an old friend was going with him, but no details. When his sister Brigit got home, she'd dig until she was satisfied with her knowledge of this "old friend," and no one knew if Justin was going to make it back for the wedding.

"This might be Dillon and Elle's big day," Cash said, "but it's kicking off a stream of weddings."

"We'll all be lucky if Brock and Josie invite us to their nuptials."

The other two snorted in agreement.

Cash adjusted his hat. "Did your mom ever hit you up with potential dates for the wedding?"

Travis groaned. "No." That scared him more than if she'd had. The hurdle of getting them to accept the daughter of their cantankerous neighbor was high enough, but to fend off his mom's ideas of perfect mates was an unknown obstacle. He'd left for college and then met Michelle. Mom hadn't needed to set him up.

How tenacious was she going to be?

Dillon scuffed his boot against the ground. "I'm guessing

since you've been skipping around the farm that Kami made your day when she said yes?"

Travis grinned. Today was the day they went officially public. He could show her off, dance with her, and finally feel what it was like to be a real couple with her. His family would have to take them seriously no matter who Kami's parents were.

Travis sauntered away. "Mom and Dad are going to grill me about Kami and that's a whole 'nother mess after all the stunts her dad pulled."

Cash shook his head. "Old Man English was an ornery bastard. He was always on Dad about the cattle pushing his fences down. As if we didn't repair them constantly because he never took care of them. I never understood why Pam didn't leave his ass. He couldn't have been a good husband. Or father."

Travis scowled. Kami had never delved into the subject. She'd been a daddy's girl, but that didn't mean he'd been warm and nurturing.

Dillon *tsked*. "You mean like why she was always looking for approval from men. We all know nothing was good enough for Mr. English."

"She's not like that anymore," Travis snapped.

Cash and Dillon exchanged a look.

Irritation ate at Travis. "You guys don't know her. She's strong, resourceful, and committed to raising her daughter."

"We didn't say she wasn't," Dillon said cautiously. "We're on your side, and we remember how depressed you got about being stood up. We're happy for you, but we're cautious."

Cash ducked his head. "We hated leaving for basic training because you were still a wreck and trying not to show it."

They were worried about him; he got that. But he

shouldn't have to convince his entire family it wasn't a bad idea.

He couldn't leave without making his point. "You all found love when you needed it the most, from the unlikeliest of places." Cash and his Army buddy's sister. Brock and the sister of the man who'd vandalized their property. Both times, his cousins had been warned about the disaster potential. "Let me and Kami find our way."

Cash pushed off the pickup. "No matter what, man. We're here for you."

"Got it. See you in a few hours." So they didn't leave on such a heavy note, he turned to Dillon. "Better go shave. She's not marrying a lumberjack."

"She likes the whiskers," Dillon replied.

Travis chuckled and climbed into his pickup. The trip home was only a few miles away. A rental car was parked by his barn.

Mom and Dad. Brigit wasn't at the house yet. Good. One inquisition at a time.

"Hey, guys," he called as he walked into his house.

"I'm in here."

He entered the kitchen. Mom was tucked into the fridge, rummaging around. His stomach circled into a knot. He knew what she'd find in there—and that she'd ask.

She straightened with an armload of containers. Inspecting one, she set the rest down on the counter. "Are these still good?"

"Yes." He didn't offer any more info.

"I have to admit, I'm a bit surprised. I told your dad we should stop and pick up a few things, but he said we could always run back to town." She grinned at him. "I think he forgets what a commute it is from here to a grocery store. In Phoenix, they're all over."

He'd never get used to his parents wandering around in

khaki shorts and polo shirts. They used to be all blue jeans and work boots, but once Dad golfed for the first time, he was lost to their new way of living.

Mom opened the container and sniffed.

"That's from Thursday. I swear you won't get sick." Kami cleaned out anything he hadn't eaten within a few days to make room for more. Rarely had he left any food behind.

She popped the lid of another container. "Meatballs?"

"Meatball subs. They were delicious."

She glanced at him. "When'd you start cooking?"

Here it goes. He might as well lay it all out there before he arrived at the wedding with Kami on his arm. "I've been helping Kami Preston with her mom's property. She insisted on repaying me, but I'd feel like a crook taking her money. We settled on food."

"Preston? Oh...Kami English." The surprise wasn't unexpected, and he waited for the rest. "She comes here and cooks?"

"Yes."

"Do you two...eat together?"

"Yes, Mom. We've started seeing each other."

"Oh." She stared blankly at the food bins in front of her.

"I know. You've had problems with her parents, but that's all in the past." He leaned against the doorframe, waiting on Mom's judgment. Because it'd always been important to him.

She nodded slowly. "Umm...how serious are you two?"

"I'd like it to go somewhere."

"She has a kid, right?"

"Kambria. She's ten."

"And what does she think?" Mom's voice was carefully even. He couldn't tell where she was going with her questions.

"She doesn't know. I've taken her riding, but that's it.

Kami doesn't want her to know, wants to be sure of us, but I'm hopeful. She's my date today."

Mom blinked at him. Her bright hazel eyes brimming with astonishment. "Oh. That was fast."

"It only seems fast because you weren't here."

Mom gingerly set the container of meatballs down and faced him. "What do you two have in common?"

Mom had loved Michelle. Each time Michelle had called it off, his mom's heart cracked just a little. *She's such a smart girl. She's so driven. So down to earth. I think you both work so well together.*

His traitorous mind clicked through all the places in the house they'd had sex. Not an appropriate answer to what they had in common. He shouldn't have to cover the same ground with his mother that he'd had to go over with Kami. He enjoyed her company—clothes on or off.

"I see." Mom grabbed three plates from a cupboard and smacked the meatballs onto one. She banged open the microwave and slid the plate inside. The *click* of the door shutting rang across the kitchen.

"Something smells delicious." Dad breezed into the room, giving him a clap on the shoulder as he passed. "Hey, I like what you did with the west quarter. That corn is huge. What's the seed?"

"It's a hybrid that I'm testing for a company out of Sioux Falls."

Mom's back was to him, but her words were clear. "Travis is seeing Earl English's daughter."

Dad's brows lifted. "Kami English?"

"Preston." Did no one pay attention to her getting married, or did they assume it wouldn't matter?

"That's right." Dad gathered utensils and exchanged a look with Mom. People did that a lot around him.

His mom sighed and looked over her shoulder. "She lost a husband. You lost—"

"I get it," he said tightly. "But we're both allowed to move on."

"I'm not worried about Kami moving on."

"Mom!"

Mom crossed her arms over her chest. "I remember how devastated you were when she stood you up. And not more than a year after that, she was married."

"We were kids."

"What your mom is saying…" Dad exchanged a look with Mom.

Travis pushed off the wall. "We're both allowed to grow up, and we're both allowed to move on."

"Well, I talked to Sheila Yager to see if we could meet for coffee while I was here. You remember her daughter, Amelia? She's a pharmacist in town."

Drop it, Mom. "I do. I'm not interested."

"You might find that you two have more in common. I put in a good word. Amelia's around all weekend. She's a pharmacist."

Frustration churned in his gut. "You said that."

"You should think about it."

"Why? I'm a farmer; she's a pharmacist. What are we going to talk about over dinner? How antibiotic supplemented feed correlates with the incidence of antibiotic resistant organisms infecting humans? Should I ask her for the flu shot and out to a movie, and then comment on how many calves I helped Cash vaccinate?"

Mom blinked. "Yes. Exactly. Try asking Kami English those questions and see how long you two can talk."

"Wow, Mom." He left the kitchen, his appetite gone.

"Just think about it is all I'm asking," Mom called. "How's your next computer game coming?"

His shoulders tensed. "I haven't been working on it."

"But you had the design all planned out. Haven't you started programming? I told everyone in Phoenix that you'd have it ready by the end of the year."

"I've been busy. I gotta shower." Veering into his room, he swung the door shut after him. Sinking onto the edge of his bed, he released a long sigh.

Well, that was over with.

~

KAMI TURNED TO THE LEFT. To the right. And back.

How the hell was someone supposed to dress for a wedding?

She'd been too deep in kid-raising—and she'd never been invited. Keeping girlfriends had been hard. Impossible after she moved. Right when she was creating solid friendships, or so she thought, Ben died and they'd drifted away after a few consoling words.

The excuse that she was essentially new to town worked for a while. Now a year had passed and she was still friendless.

Her coworkers helped her stay sane, but they were as interested in socializing as they were in underwater basket-weaving.

When she'd gotten married, she walked down the aisle in her mom's dress. An ivory, off-the-shoulder sheath dress.

Mom had worn the dress and Dad had died. Kami had worn the dress and Ben had died.

After she'd moved back, she and Mom had a special bonding moment when they'd burned that dress. Kambria had asked what they were toasting to. A better beginning.

She grimaced. None of her reminiscing was helping now.

An A-line sleeveless dress with a muted floral pattern.

Not too flashy, not too bright. Not white. Not black. A pair of strappy sandals and she'd kill it.

Chewing on her lip, she studied her reflection. She'd had to buy a new outfit. The only dress she owned was the one she buried Ben in, and she cried whenever she looked at it. It'd get incinerated in the next bonfire.

She was going out. With Travis Walker. His family and the whole town would know.

Oh god! Mom!

She found her phone and dialed. As soon as her mom answered, she let her news spill out. "I'm going on a date with Travis Walker and I really like him."

Silence greeted her. "And you think I'll be pissed."

"Yes."

Mom sighed. "I'm not thrilled about his parents, and if Travis ever treats you like they did us, then I'll have a problem. Until then, you're and adult and he's not Austin, so go on. Have fun."

She held a hand to her forehead. Was it a sign she was growing up or regressing when she asked for her mom's permission? No, it'd been more of a blessing.

She jumped at the knock on the door. Travis.

She rushed to answer the door, pausing to step into her sandals.

Oh shit. The tags were still on. She'd forgotten.

"Just a minute." Stupid price tag. She ripped it off and stuffed it into the trash. It shouldn't be a big deal if Travis new she'd had to do an emergency shopping trip. Until yesterday, she could've sworn that she was going to cancel.

Ending the night in Travis's arms and then sneaking home to an empty apartment had her pondering what she was getting into. The wedding was a turning point. She'd arrive on Travis's muscular arm knowing every inch of what he looked like naked. They'd mingle. His family would have to talk to her. If they didn't, then she'd know there was trouble in their future.

But if the night was enjoyable and maybe even not awkward, she and Travis could be the real thing. A couple.

And she'd have to tell Kambria. Would her personality switch like it had on Austin?

That wasn't a worry for tonight.

She feathered her hands over her hair to tame any strays. Her long locks hung in a sleek wave. She patted her dress down for no damn reason.

Open the door!

She whipped it wide.

Travis's extremely capable lips curved into a smile and his gaze licked her from head to toe.

"You're stunning."

Her face warmed. Because *day-um*. Put the man in a black pair of jeans with shiny black boots… Her heart stammered. Cowboy boots, not his usual work boots. His crisp white button-up shirt draped over his wide shoulders and set his blue eyes aglow.

"Do you have a hat to go with those boots?" Her voice nearly shook.

His eyes sparkled with humor. "We don't do cowboys hats. They don't fit in the tractor. And we don't do sport coats, either, because it's over eighty degrees." He held his arm out. "Ready?"

If she said no, it'd ruin the night. She and her belly full of raving butterflies would endure.

"Did your family make it down okay?"

His bicep flexed under her hand. She glanced at him, but his expression was neutral. "They're here. Justin rolled in a few minutes before I left. Late as always. Brigit stayed in town to meet up with friends before the wedding. Mom and Dad are at the church already."

Yay… Everyone would be there. This could be a giant debacle, or a really great night.

He led her to his pickup. The midnight blue paint sparkled under the sunlight. Freshly washed. When they were both inside, her stomach lurched as he threw it in drive.

The church was on the other side of downtown, but it was Moore, and the trip took about five minutes. She steadied her hand on the door. Her nerves made her want to jump out and run back to her apartment.

When had she ever been nervous for a date?

He offered his arm again. She cradled her hand in the crook of his elbow and they walked up the sidewalk to the arched wooden doorway of the hundred-year-old stone church. One side of the door opened. A young woman swept out, her hand on her forehead.

"Something wrong, Brigit?"

Kami looked closer at the girl. *That* was Travis's sister? She was a good five years younger than them and would've barely been a teenager when Kami last saw her. Gone was the ruddy-faced little girl with wild hair that bested a brush on a normal day. Brigit Walker was a few inches taller than her, with a full, curvy body and short, styled hair that was dyed the softest shade of lavender.

She dropped her hand. Brigit won the body lotto and hit the looks jackpot. Keen eyes latched onto her and Travis. At first they seemed blue, but a ring of yellow around the irises made them impossibly bright. Kami used to wish her eye color was as vibrant instead of wet dirt-road brown.

"Nope, it's all fine. Kami, hi." Brigit stuck her hand out. "Remember me?"

Kami gave it a quick shake, some of her nerves fading at Brigit's open greeting. "Of course. I can't forget the girl who brought a frog onto the bus."

Brigit's eyes widened, like the memory hit her out of left

field, then she grinned, her mega-watt smile blinding. "It wasn't bringing the frog on the bus that was the issue, it was losing it."

Travis chuckled. "If only a frog was the tamest thing you tried to bring."

Brigit waved toward the church. "They're all inside. I'll be back in a bit." She wandered away.

They entered the church. Kami blinked. After the glare of a summer afternoon, everything was dark. She kept her gaze down and let Travis guide her to the front rows.

"There are no assigned sides for family," he spoke low into her ear, his breath giving her delicious shivers. "Elle doesn't have much for family; just her dad will be here. The ceremony will be small and intimate. The reception is what they've invited others to."

They neared the group and a moment of unease disturbed her stomach. She pressed a hand to it. The reception would've been a better place to bring her. He was right. The sizable group was small for a wedding, and the atmosphere was more intimate and familiar than she'd anticipated.

I can do this.

Several pairs of eyes watched them approach. She smiled hesitantly—she hoped. It could be a grimace the way her insides were turning like she was doing round-off after round-off.

Cash greeted her first and she could've hugged him for it.

His fiancée stepped forward and introduced herself next. "I'm guessing you know everybody already. We didn't quite get introduced at the street dance. I'm Abbi. You remember Elle?" Kami nodded. "Then you haven't officially met Josie, either?"

A young woman stepped forward. Kami guessed both Abbi and Josie were a few years younger than her. Josie's gaze was as assessing as the rest of them, but was filled with more curiosity than anything.

The round of introductions was quick. If pressed, she could've deciphered what set of parents went with what Walker kid, but they all reintroduced themselves.

The handshake from Travis's mom was as cool as her gaze. His dad's wasn't much better. Her stomach went from nervous flutter to outright heartburn. Meeting Justin, his brother, wasn't any different than greeting Brock or Aaron. Like his twin sister, he seemed distracted.

Aaron's younger brothers looked like scrawnier versions of him. All three of them were in sharp black jeans and white dress shirts. Same with the other guys. Only Travis's dad wore khaki slacks that looked like they belonged on a golf course.

A slender man she didn't recognize appeared. He shuffled carefully across the floor. The closer he came, the easier it was to see that he was probably in the age range of the other parents. He must be Elle's dad.

"They're getting started. Have a seat, everyone. Thanks for coming." He continued his path to the back of the church where Elle waited for him in a simple, but elegant white dress.

Within seconds, they were all seated. As if an unspoken suggestion had been made, they covered both sides of the aisle so it didn't look like Elle's side was empty. Kami's impression of the Walkers went up another notch. If she ever married into this family, Mom and Kambria would be her lone family members. She almost snorted. That was one more than she had when she married Ben. Only his family hadn't surrounded her in support. Mom had been alone with a few town stragglers that filed in after her and sat on the bride's side because there was no room left on the Preston side.

A fresh wave of bitterness crashed into her. Someday, she'd have to let that go.

But not while her in-laws manipulated her daughter's summer.

Travis squeezed her hand as if he sensed her negative feelings. She smiled at him and forced herself to pay attention to the vows being murmured back and forth.

Nope. She couldn't do it. Memories assaulted her of her bittersweet big day. If it hadn't been for Ben's calming effect and solidarity, she would've abandoned him at the altar and waddled her pregnant ass out of town as fast as she could. And ultimately, that's why she stayed. To have that kind of support and encouragement and unabashed devotion from a man was more than she'd ever hoped for.

Because she hadn't been naive. Dad hadn't been an easy man to stand by. Her parents' almost adversarial relationship wasn't a fitting example of wedded bliss.

What would it be like to marry Travis? Of course, she was waaaay ahead of herself, but just for fun, what-if? Would he be as committed to them as Ben had been? Because that'd been as intoxicating as that first taste of lust. Some of the splendor had worn off the longer Ben hadn't stood up for her to his parents or his siblings. He'd stood with her, and as the years passed, she realized they were different. He'd been a peace-keeper and that'd been enough—at first, until she'd started wishing he'd say more to his family.

Rowdy applause yanked her out of her thoughts. Dillon and Elle were sharing a kiss. The ceremony was over. She'd be relieved, but this was the easy part.

CHAPTER 12

*P*eople piled into the dance hall. Kami sat at a table next to Travis. Justin was on his other side, and his parents and Brigit were across from them. Kami slowly inhaled a deep breath and just as slowly released it. Her appetite had vanished as soon as Joan and Rick Walker arrived.

She pushed her potato salad around, gave up, and placed her fork next to her plate.

The decorations in the place had a simple yet sophisticated quality, transforming the area from a plain, square room with an outdated feel to a cozy reception. As more and more well-wishers arrived, and the louder it became, it lost the intimate air that the wedding had. Each Walker family had their own table and she doubted Elle or Dillon would be seen the rest of the night. Every time one group of people broke away from them, another formed.

Kami scanned the rest of the place. She'd spent so many weekends in here, with various guys she had dated. As she watched the crowd, her mouth quirked. Nothing changed.

After a certain time of night, it was still generally accepted that the invitation was open to all.

"I'm sorry, did you say something?" Joan asked.

Was she talking to her? Kami glanced over. Oh shit. Yes, Joan was looking at her. "No?"

Travis pushed his plate aside and reclined, laying his arm across the back of her chair. "You were smiling. I think she thought she missed something."

Did she? Or was Joan putting her on the spot? "I was marveling over how some things never change." She nodded toward the dance floor. "Like how many kids are going to show up just to party."

"Is that what you did?" Joan's tone had an edge disguised in innocence.

Brigit rolled her eyes. "Please, Mom. That's what we all did."

Joan shot her a patronizing look. "Did you, dear? I had hoped you and your friends were studying like you said you were."

"We did. Then we hit the dance."

"I hope you didn't do that in college."

Brigit blew out an exasperated sigh. "Yes, I did. And that's exactly why I didn't get into med school." Her voice dripped sarcasm. She grabbed her champagne glass and left the table.

Kami leaned into Travis's side as if she could disappear, make them forget she was there.

"I guess that answers that question," Travis said. "She didn't get in."

Rick shook his head. "She was on the waiting list, but they didn't make it to her number."

"I told her to apply again." Worry lines fanned out from Joan's eyes. "She isn't saying if she will or won't."

Why'd it matter? Brigit had the fortitude to apply to med

school, it was unlikely she'd settle for an everyday job. And if she did, so what?

Joan switched her focus. Kami shifted so she sat straighter. A little voice in her head said, *Here we go.*

"And what was it you did again, Kami?"

"I wait tables at Old Main and when I don't have Kambria I pick up bartending shifts at Tyler's Club." She held Joan's gaze, didn't miss the glint of disapproval. Joan and Martha could be friends.

"What'd you go to school for?"

"I didn't." Keeping her tone light, she smiled as the earlier moment of nostalgia faded. "Unlike Travis, school wasn't for me."

Travis squeezed her shoulder. "Not everyone wants to endure years of dry lectures."

Her half-hearted chuckle covered her shame. She'd love to, but she couldn't pass the tests.

Joan glanced between the two of them, her mouth flat. "And your daughter, you said you don't always have her?"

Travis adjusted in his seat. Was he going to cut his mom's questions off? Because no one else was. They were content to let Joan Walker grill her.

"Kambria's grandparents live in Normandy and they try to spend a lot of time with her. They finagled a six-week gymnastics camp together this summer."

Joan's eyebrows lifted. "How nice. Six weeks to yourself."

A flash of anger coursed through her at the snide lilt to her statement. "No, it sucks. I don't like being away from Kambria."

Justin excused himself. She envied his ability to leave. She could, too, but that'd make no progress with Mama Bear.

A moment of irritation at Travis floated up, but she quashed it down. She'd be offended if he felt he had to defend her against Mama Joan. In a way, his silence showed that he didn't think she had anything to defend herself for.

She hoped, because right now, a vision of her in front of a well-dressed firing squad emerged. "I wouldn't want to go through this life without her. I miss her, but she loves gymnastics as much as I did."

Travis tucked her in close. A show of support? "I don't think I've talked to her without seeing her do a cartwheel or five. She's a great kid."

Joan's pinched gaze danced between them. Kami's lungs froze waiting for a comment, but Rick spoke first. "Did the academy in town close?"

Kami nodded. "Five years ago. The owner moved away and no one else was willing to run it." She shrugged. "The hours are mostly evening because of the sessions and the owner should have comprehensive knowledge of how to run a recreational and competitive program."

"I'm sure a solid business acumen is also necessary. I can't imagine it's easy to find both."

Was that a dig at gymnastics? A general speculation? The former owner had been a huge mentor to her and all the other coaches. She'd also had an MBA. If it wasn't for Kami's old boss's encouragement, she wouldn't have gotten involved in the Normandy program and gotten a piece of herself back after childbirth.

If it wasn't for her mentor's help, she wouldn't have gathered all the data she had and been prepared to open her own gym.

She could tell Joan all of that, but she didn't. She could pull up her files from the app on her phone and prove to Martha that she'd put together a stable, sensible plan with only a diploma.

What would be the point? It's why she'd kept it secret until she'd had to abandon it.

Abandonment of her hopes and dreams had seemed inevitable. Those plans would stay saved because she'd never know if she would've failed at it. The unknown would be a source of comfort as she trudged out in snow to check on stinky sheep.

Rick interrupted her thoughts and said exactly what she'd thought when she'd heard the gym was closing its doors. "It was a loss for the community when it closed." He turned to Joan. "It looks like the dance is starting soon. Think we still got it in us?"

Joan smiled. "You know we do."

They both left the table. Watching Joan interact with Rick made her seem human. But the frosty conversation prior wasn't enough to warm her up to Travis's mom.

"Well, that was fun," she said flatly.

Travis looked partially contrite. "I'm sorry. I didn't want to insult you by answering for you."

So it hadn't been because he was ashamed. A question popped into her mind but she debated a moment before asking. "Was she like that with Michelle?"

Travis stilled, his gaze planted on the table. "At first."

He answered so carefully, there had to be a reason. Between Joan's pointed questions and the drama with Brigit, she figured out why. "Michelle was the educated girl she wanted for you."

He swiveled to face her. "Trust me when I tell you that how much schooling or how big of a degree you have doesn't matter." He clenched his jaw as he seemed to work through what he was going to say. "Sometimes, I felt like that was all Michelle and I had in common."

She didn't know much about his relationship with his fiancée, but this was the first she'd heard there was anything less than optimistic bliss.

The music kicked off a fun country beat. She met Travis's gaze and they both smiled.

"Dillon said the only plan for tonight was to dance and have fun." He tipped his head toward the dance floor where Dillon spun his mom around. "It'd make them both uncomfortable to have the spotlight on them for special dances."

Kami interpreted that as it'd make Elle uncomfortable. From what she remembered of Dillon, he was just fine front and center, commanding attention. Elle's dad had looked frail, yet excited, and a special father/daughter spin might've have been too much for him.

Kami's foot started tapping to the beat. Travis noticed immediately.

"I missed my chance with you at the street dance. How 'bout now?"

His mom was forgotten. His entire family left her mind. After a few seconds in his arms, the rest of the dance hall faded away.

The man could move, and after the last few weeks together, they were as in sync fully clothed as they were without a stitch. Kami laughed in delight as he spun and twirled her. They danced around couples, through them, all across the floor, didn't matter the type of song. She wished she packed her cowboy boots for the night.

As the night went on, she and Travis traded partners until she'd danced with every Walker of the Walker Five and their younger siblings. The parents had all migrated to the tables and their rowdy guffaws often rose over the volume of the DJ.

The final song of the night was announced and she was back in Travis's arms.

He dipped his head down to her hair as they circled in harmony with the few remaining dancers. She was well aware of the looks they'd drawn from the crowd throughout the night. If it wasn't clear they were dating after this, it'd have to be spelled out.

Who and how many people would care was the question. When it came to her with someone other than Austin, it was always downturned mouths and snotty comments. After Dad died, Mom had gotten the same reaction when she'd started dating. Only she hadn't had the benefit of an old boyfriend to return to. Would Joan have thought twice about her if she'd arrived with Austin? Or would they be deemed "right for each other"?

"Can I stay at your place tonight?" His words in her ear made her shiver and forget the path her thoughts were taking.

She nodded, cuddling in closer. As the music died down, someone tapped her shoulder.

Cash cradled a flushed and grinning Abbi in his arms. "Monday's hay day, remember."

Smiling, she said, "I remember."

Cash leaned close to Travis, Abbi giggling and squished between them. "Do everything I'd do."

Travis threw her a heated looked.

Cash swaggered away, but Abbi's loud whisper was perfectly clear. "I think they already have."

"I guess I have to go prove them right." Travis towed her with him through the stragglers, some faces she knew, some she didn't. His hand was closed around hers, his actions proprietary, and she was in touch with her feminine side enough to admit that she liked it.

If only he'd acted the same around his parents.

TRAVIS AIMED the tractor down another row to swath. He'd volunteered to help Cash with Hay Day Monday. Kami was working and wouldn't be around, but he wanted to help in some way. He and Cash would cut the pastures and let them dry out, then come back to bale. They'd do it all while Kami was working, so she didn't have to worry about a thing. She was already giving them a great deal on the bales since they were haying, and they didn't have the extra cost of gas to haul across the county.

His phone pinged.

Are your parents still at your place?

Instead of fumbling with the phone while steering, he called her back. The tractor had an enclosed cab, and while it was nosier than a car, he could still talk. He'd spent the morning on the old tractor Cash was using before they switched. It didn't have a cab, letting the sun beat down in the summer and the wind chafe them raw during every other season. The newer, more expensive red Case tractor was bigger and stored at his place, so he'd just drive it home when he was done. Cash could cut through the pastures to get home.

After a couple of rings, she answered.

"I figured it'd be easier to call." He took a deep breath. "Yes, they're not leaving until tomorrow."

"Then I'll let you visit before they leave. Are you in the field?"

"I'm in *your* field." He infused his voice with suggestion, then dropped back to normal after her breathy laugh. "I don't want you scared away from my parents. Come over for supper."

"I...can't."

"Is it my mom?"

"Is it obvious?"

Yeah, he'd fucked up this weekend. Mom had adored Michelle and it hadn't helped his relationship with her. He was adult enough to know that his mom and Kami getting along would make a relationship easier, but it wasn't critical.

Although it could be if he didn't handle it properly. "You're coming over, and you're not cooking. Dad took out a massive amount of steaks to grill."

Her end was quiet.

Damn. Waking up to Kami yesterday morning after the dance was the best experience he'd had in…ever. It was everything he'd hoped and more. She'd stood him up for that date all those years ago, but she hadn't this weekend. He was determined to have her. She was all that was missing in his life.

"Kami, I want you over. Though I can't promise it'll be fun, I can promise that I'll be with you. I love my mother, adore her, but she has no say about you and I."

"You're making a good case for supper."

Her tone was dry, but there was a smile in her voice. This might actually work.

"I'm serious about you, Kami. About us."

"Me, too," she said softly. "What time?"

He grinned and rattled off the information and hung up. It pinged again.

Without looking, he answered. "I swear, it'll be okay."

"Travis? Did I call at a bad time?"

Shiiiit. Michelle's dad. His hand fisted around his phone. Why hadn't he checked the screen? "Apologies, Phil. I thought you were my…cousin." Travis grimaced. What a fucking liar.

"Della and I are on vacation this week and we wondered when would be a good time to visit."

His heart pounded. He steered the tractor the best he could while only half his attention was on the task. Why hadn't he sprung for the Bluetooth? Because he'd spent too much time on his electronics and he could go days with no calls, just his cousins texting back and forth.

"My parents are here tonight, but they leave tomorrow. Any time's fine. Just shoot me a message first." The idea of being surprised by Michelle's parents while he was cementing plans for a future with Kami sent stomach acid clawing up his esophagus. They'd need time to be told first, to process it.

"Will do, Travis. And thank you." The sorrow in the man's voice… He wanted to shut his eyes against it, but crashing a fence wouldn't help either of them. He'd have to give Kami a heads up that he might have company one night and she'd get the night off. Then he'd have to talk to her about why he'd procrastinated about telling Phil and Della that he'd started dating again. She'd understand their pain, no doubt, but she wouldn't know the guilt that festered inside of him.

The haying done, he ambled home. Dad jogged out of the house to help him unload the attachment and park the tractor in the shop. Travis relayed his plans for the night.

Dad was hesitant. "She's coming over tonight? Your mother might be kind of disappointed. She didn't feel like we got to visit much with you over the weekend."

Yeah, he spent Sunday morning cradled in Kami's lush body and the afternoon welding a busted gate in his horse pasture. But Mom had never complained about Michelle coming over, or if he'd been in Fargo when they came to visit.

"Well, I'm here all night," Travis said with a note of finality in his voice. "And Kami is my guest."

He and his dad finished and walked together back to the house. Nothing more was said about Kami, and that was unusual for his dad. He'd always asked about Michelle. The thing with Kami was new. Travis had to remember that his parents had known about her half a week. He couldn't expect them to act the same way about her as they did with Michelle.

He ran through the shower and stepped into a clean pair of Wranglers and a fresh shirt. Buttoning the last button, he jerked when the doorbell rang.

When was the last time Kami had rang the doorbell? She had a key. He hated their act of not being as familiar with each other as they were, should've told her to just come in.

Mom beat him to the door. She was cool with Kami, and his woman's rigid posture and tightly clasped hands sent alarms through him. He sidled next to her and slid his arm around her waist.

Mom held up a wine bottle and inspected the label. "Strawberry rhubarb. Where'd you say it was from?"

"A winery outside of Fargo. I like to try each flavor."

"Hmm. Well, thank you." Mom took off for the kitchen without another word.

Kami shot him a wide-eyed look. "Did I do something wrong?"

"Not at all. I think you catch her off guard." And not in a good way, but at least Mom was civil.

"Brigit and Justin left already?"

"Yesterday." He threaded his fingers through hers and led her after his mom. "It's just us."

They both smiled, but the same tension from the wedding was back between them.

Mom immersed herself in meal prep while he idly chatted with Kami. Her furtive glances toward his parents broke his heart. She'd mentioned her in-laws behavior toward her. Was she scared his parents would repeat it?

The actual meal simmered with animosity. He tried to share various bits of information about Kami with his parents, but his mom's cold demeanor doused most of his attempts.

Somehow, he'd make this up to Kami.

Mom set down her fork, her expression neutral. "When do you think you'll have Farmland Two out?"

She'd already asked. Where was she going with this? "I don't know. I've been a little busy, and designing the first game was a hobby to fill my time." Because Michelle had come down to Moore less and less often. "Maybe this winter I'll revisit my plans."

"You were so proud when you released the first one. I don't want to see you lose momentum." Her gaze strayed to Kami for a fraction of a second. "I'd hate for you to distract yourself until you forget what's really important."

The atmosphere in the dining room grew heavy. Kami placed her napkin on the table and folded her hands in her lap. Her back ramrod straight, it was like she'd been through this before. Knowing her dad and the tirades Travis had witnessed between his own dad and Earl English, she probably had. Nothing had ever been good enough for Earl. He'd held everyone up to an unreasonably high standard while his own standards were flushable.

His mom was not Earl, neither should she act like it. "I'm not distracting myself. Building games is a hobby. Hobbies are for when you have nothing else to do. I have other things to do and people I want to be around."

He wanted to say more, but never in his life had he told off his mother, and he didn't want to start now. They could be civil. Adults.

They'd always been so open about how proud of him they were. Disappointing them was akin to causing physical pain. He left the attitudes and flippant statements up to his siblings. He'd been Mom's reprieve; the good kid. He'd have to tread carefully to keep from hurting both his mom and Kami.

Mom eyed him evenly. "I don't want to see you make a

mistake with something so important." Her words clearly said she wasn't talking about a game.

Kami watched him, her lips pressed together.

"Trust me, Mom. Everything's okay."

"And the research collaboration with the extension office? Are you helping author any papers?"

Travis shrugged. "I might be listed in the acknowledgements when they publish on the new corn seed we've tested for them. I got a call last week from an old graduate school buddy on how useful I might find a drone and if I was willing to help test one out. We meet next week."

"Drones." Rick snorted. "Back when I started with my dad, having AC was a luxury."

Kami shot him an odd look, a mixture of curiosity and hurt. He'd have to ask about it when they were alone.

His mom smiled. "I can't imagine them calling anyone else to help with their research. How are Phil and Della?" She switched her attention to Kami. "Did he tell you how much he helps them? Poor dears. Losing Michelle destroyed them. Their grief would have taken their business down if it wasn't for Travis."

Travis smiled and seized on the subject change, even if it wasn't the one his mom had meant. "And you wonder why I don't have to time design a game."

"What do you do for them?" Kami asked, her voice soft.

"The planning. Phil's running on autopilot right now. He's getting there, but he needed my help." Probably still needed him, but Travis could talk to Kami about that later. "How'd your in-laws do after Ben died?"

Mom folded her hands on the table but stayed quiet. Her gaze was serious, respectful. He hadn't meant to use Ben's death to legitimize Kami in his mom's eyes. Phil had taken it so hard, Travis was understandably curious about how others dealt with the death of an adult child.

"As well as you could imagine. Everyone's different, I suppose. They had a lot of support, a lot of love. I won't lie that having Kambria around was huge in helping them through the worst of the grief. They get to see a little of him in her every time she visits."

His mom smiled, but he couldn't tell how sincere it was. "They must want her to visit a lot."

"Quite often, yes." Kami didn't elaborate. "It's all I can do to keep them from monopolizing her time." Kami's tone was light; the undercurrent of bitterness was probably only apparent to him. "They were distraught when I told them I was moving, but it was almost like living with overprotective parents. My only goal is to give my daughter the opportunity for experiences that I had. That includes a bigger space to live and run, a place where we can have some animals. It means the world to raise her where I grew up. It means the world to me that she sees me doing what I love, or working hard to achieve it. I couldn't do that in Normandy."

He studied his parents' reaction. Dad was more at ease, but that's how he usually was. He'd been reserved tonight, limiting his additions to their conversation. Mom's expression had softened. His parents needed time to drop their idea of how perfect he and Michelle had been so they could see that Kami wasn't her father or mother, or even the girl who had once broken his heart.

He wanted to stress how much more alike he and Kami were than him and Michelle. "I can empathize. Moving back from Fargo couldn't come soon enough. I was born here, and I'm gonna stay here."

Mom chuckled. "This house has built quite the family legacy. I'm glad it's in good hands."

Kami cast him a look he couldn't decipher.

His dad rested his elbows on the table. "What are you planning to do with your mom's place, Kami?"

Kami glanced at Travis, her gaze wary. "I'm concentrating on going through Dad's things and seeing what I have to work with. The sale won't be final until the end of summer, so I'm taking inventory and making plans."

Why wasn't she sharing her sheep ranching plans?

"Any thoughts on what you'd put in the pasture?" Dad asked.

"I have lots of thoughts, but I'd like to take time and be thorough before I implement any ideas. This is not just my future, but my daughter's."

She avoided looking at Travis. Had she changed her mind? Regardless, he followed her lead and didn't mention the excellent ranching plan she'd written up.

Mom stood. "Well, Travis was thoughtful enough to have frozen some rhubarb before it got woody. I made some rhubarb custard bars. Perhaps it will pair well with your wine."

The mood lifted. Kami's relieved smile was real. Travis sat back, fighting a grin. Kami had gone to the wedding with him and his parents were willing to give Kami a chance, however tentatively.

This was all working out well.

CHAPTER 13

Tuesday dragged on. Kami waited tables, bussed them, and during the afternoon slump, filled ketchup bottles, all with her thoughts stuck on the previous night. They'd had a breakthrough of sorts. By the end of the night, Travis's parents were more relaxed around her, more open during their conversation. Rick had peppered her with questions about her mom's property as if he'd been dying to know the state of it since her dad had passed away.

She couldn't blame him. Rick Walker had often suffered the wrath of Dad. Anything and everything that had gone wrong on the not-quite-working ranch, Dad had found a reason to blame the Walkers. Cash's dad had gotten his share, but since Rick and Joan had lived closer, they were easier targets—other than her and her mom. She'd grown up with tirade after tirade and Mom's frosty silence. *Earl, you're going to fret yourself into the ground.*

And he had.

Rick Walker wasn't faultless in the fights, but he treated her better than she'd ever witnessed him treating her dad, and that was a start. Just like Joan being almost pleasant was a huge improvement.

And Travis had played both sides as flawlessly as Ben had.

She rubbed her temples. Did she want more of the same of what she and Ben had? Or did she want Travis to put his foot down and tell his mom in no uncertain terms that she could not treat his girlfriend that way? Or was she really wishing she'd have the lady balls to tell Joan to stuff it, treat her respectfully or don't talk to her at all?

Kami dropped her hands. Her workday was over. She said goodbye to her coworkers and meandered to the backroom to clock out, grateful to leave the overwhelming smell of grease and coffee behind. If only Dad could see her now. What would he say? That she should do better. What was the point of waiting tables if she could manage the restaurant? Kind of like what was the point of barrel racing if you didn't place? After her first competition, he'd filled in the home-made barrel arena he'd erected and trashed the barrels. Or sold them. Hell, they could be buried in that decrepit barn.

Everyone thought she'd pick up racing again after he died, but it all had been his idea in the first place. Good thing she had talent and determination for gymnastics, and Mom's adamant insistence that she participate in an activity not related to school. *It'll do her some good, build her confidence.* Mom had stood firm on that but not much else.

Clocking out, Kami embraced the swell of excitement at the reminder that she was going to Travis's to make supper. The feeling wasn't as strong as it'd been in the past. She kept going back to how he'd easily diverted the conversation instead of calling out Joan's behavior. But their relationship was so young. Was she being unfair to expect so much so soon?

There was a bright side. Hiding it was no longer neces-sary, though. She and Travis could go on real dates. She had no reason to think he was ashamed of being seen with her after the wedding and dining with his family. Or that this thing between them, the raging chemistry, was anything other than a fluke, or an excuse for him to drown his heartache.

Her smile died as she trudged to the parking lot. He hadn't talked about Michelle much. Did he even notice all the pressure his mom put on him? The games. The research collaborations. The drones. At one point, Kami wondered if dating Michelle had been Joan's idea.

She'd ask about Michelle tonight. It was time for him to open up. Their relationship was more than sex, but he kept a part of him closed off from her. Like, drones? How cool! Yet he hadn't mentioned a thing.

Did he think she wasn't smart enough to understand?

The drive out to his place was an exercise in moving meditation. Rows of lush green poplars and cottonwoods alternated with evergreens to create the shelter belts that broke the wind between fields. Crops that ranged from corn to soybeans to sunflowers surrounded her. She passed Cash's place and Dillon's across the road. Dillon's side was surrounded by trees, and cattle roamed the pastures around Cash's place, with a section just for the horses. She spotted Mandrell, but Reba and Crystal Gale were at Travis's place. Brock's area was quiet, the old red barn rising above the trees around his place.

The long road ended in a loop reminiscent of a cul de sac. Aaron's driveway disappeared into his own trees that protected the property from the bitter north wind that blew through the land all winter. She turned into Travis's drive.

The two men couldn't be more different. Both good-looking, but Aaron's constant rumpled state was at odds with Travis's preppy farm boy look. She'd seen a different side of Aaron at the wedding. He could clean up as handsome as his cousins, his easy grin making him the more approachable one. Funny how she'd gone to school with all of them, only Travis was in her grade, but he'd been the only Walker she was attracted to. She knew the others through sports and bus rides, heard what the girls giggled about, but Travis had caught her eye and kept it.

Letting herself into the house, she swore.

Zero meals were planned for the week. She'd been so eager to get here, she hadn't thought about ingredients or groceries. The stress of the wedding, the event itself, and the following day of basking in Travis's undivided attention prevented her from planning anything about this week other than showing up.

In the kitchen, she rummaged through cabinets and the fridge. Joan had left Travis with enough leftovers for both of them tonight. She pulled out the chicken and pasta and dished some onto plates.

The familiar rumble of Travis's truck was clear in the kitchen. All she had to do was nuke a couple of plates. They'd wait. She abandoned the food on the counter and slipped her shoes back on. Listening close, she followed the sounds of his truck to the shop at the farthest loop of his driveway.

"Hey." She called loud enough to be heard over the drone of his diesel engine.

He popped out from around the Ford. "Oh, hey." Glancing down at himself, he held his arms out wide. "I'm not really presentable."

She'd disagree. In dusty jeans, even dustier work boots, and a green T-shirt that had smears of black across it, he looked like he should be on a poster. "I think I'll live."

She sauntered into the shop. The place was as immaculate as a shop could be. A nice, poured cement floor, with clean metal walls; the fluorescent lights chased all the shadows away. How much did something like this cost? Had they done any of the work themselves, or hired it out? Because she'd have to hire out and it'd probably cost as much as the purchase of the land.

Add in the cost of demolition of the old barn and tiny shack of a shop her dad had kept, and she was screwed six ways from Saturday. She couldn't ranch a damn thing without a shelter.

A worry for another day. A major consideration, but her optimism and determination were fading fast, and she couldn't dwell on it.

Travis fell in step beside her as she wandered around with building envy. "I'm getting the tractor ready for raking tomorrow."

Oh, the haying. "Because it's supposed to rain tonight."

"We'll rake the rows to dry and it should be ready to bale by the weekend."

The bales would bring in a little cash, but not enough to cover any of the major work she had to do. But it was a start. Fall was a popular month for weddings, and she could pick up some bartending shifts for the receptions. The extra time away from Kambria tore at her heart, went against her sole purpose for trying to make a successful ranch.

"What's wrong?"

She smiled up at him. They'd ended up at the tractor. The red piece of equipment towered over her, much larger than anything her dad had ever owned. The comparison of the two operations was disheartening. Before Travis and his cousins took over, their business was a testament to both industries—farming and ranching. Now, it outshone anything in the county and competed with the lucrative sugar beet farmers in the Red River Valley.

"I'm contemplating things."

"Like what?" He pivoted to face her. "Us?"

"A little." She stepped into his embrace, her face buried

against his chest. His scent wrapped around her. The smell of exhaust and the field and man more alluring than his shower-fresh smell, which was its own aphrodisiac. "The drone thing sounds cool. How come you didn't mention it?"

"Ah. I would've gotten around to it, but you don't grill me like my mom."

That was for sure. "Speaking of that, how do you think last night went?"

"I think we made progress."

She pulled back enough to look at him. "Are you satisfied with that?"

There was no reservation in his expression. "I think it won't be long before they know how wonderful you are. I think you impressed them with how you handled yourself. I think you would've impressed them more if you told Dad about the sheep."

"Really?" The thought had crossed her mind, followed by no fucking way would she share with Rick Walker what her idea was. Fears that he'd challenge her like he had her dad stopped her.

"No one can argue that it's a feasible option with the potential for solid profitability." He massaged small circles into her back. Instant relaxation. She molded into him, at the mercy of his touch.

He really thought highly of her plan. Doubts had daunted her that maybe he'd feigned interest to get into her bed. Or just because he geeked out over stuff like that didn't mean he thought she'd succeed. "You have way more confidence in me than anyone else."

"Because I think you can do anything. You're amazing. I'd run around town telling everyone, but I won't until I have your blessing. And you'll be the first I tell about the drone project after the meeting."

She laughed softly. Travis Walker thought she could do

anything, and if he thought like that then maybe she was making too big of a deal out of his parents. "I might wait on running through town."

"There's something I don't want to wait for."

The growl reverberated through his chest. It tingled its way through her belly down to her core. Two days since she'd been in his arms and it was like two weeks.

She glided her arms around his neck. "There's nothing stopping you."

"Only a good place to get you naked."

She bit her lip and looked around. Her gaze landed on the big red tractor. He quirked an eyebrow and glanced over his shoulder.

"I don't have to get completely naked," she purred.

"Up there in the hot seat, huh?" He lifted her and spun around.

Once her feet hit the ground by the steps up to the cab, she wasted no time. She'd scaled up two rungs when a hard smack landed on her ass.

She squealed and burst out laughing. "What the hell are you doing?" She paused. "Maybe you should go up first? So you can sit on the seat and I can straddle you?"

"Nah. I've got another idea."

A thrill zinged through her. She scrambled into the cab. How was this going to work? Tractor sex was a first for her. She'd done it in plenty of cars, but they had a full passenger seat and a back seat. There was a small square jump seat by the main chair. What if her leg hit the controls to her right? What if one of their limbs cracked a computer screen?

And holy shit, is this what the new equipment came with now days? Growing up, they'd bought used. No, not just used. Old and used.

Travis's footsteps on the metal rungs wiped out all her questions. Fuck it. They'd make it work. She watched him ascend, his look predatory. The gleam in his eye sent shivers up and down her spine.

"Turn around."

"How? Where?" If she twisted until she faced out the back window, there'd still be no room for him behind her.

He propped one boot on the floor of the cab. With one hand on her hip, he guided her. She turned, putting her knees on the seat.

"Put your hands on the glass if you need to. You'll have to face out the side." His voice was thick, full of desire.

Who knew that finding a good position to have sex in the cab of haying equipment would be foreplay. Her sex was ready, had settled into a steady thrum that increased the closer they got in the cab.

He caressed along her waist; her breath quickened. His expert fingers unclasped her black work slacks as he nuzzled her nape.

Her eyelids drifted shut. He tunneled his hand down to between her folds. Oh yes, she was so ready for him.

"Travis," she breathed.

"I'm right here." He shifted. He must be kneeling on the jump seat, curled over her so they both fit.

He kissed up the side of her neck to her earlobe as he worked her clit. Her hips followed the rhythm he set. She gave herself a full minute before she exploded.

Abruptly, he drew his hand out. She whimpered at the loss of contact.

"Oh, I'm not done yet." His gruff tone sent another shudder through her.

She could spend her life with this man.

Her eyes flew open. Had she really thought that?

Yes, but it wasn't so much as could she. An intelligent, kind, hard-working, incredibly sexy, understanding man wasn't a hardship. It was whether she spent her time worried he'd ditch her because she wasn't good enough. But last night had put her worries to rest. Mostly.

He tugged her pants down. His zipper could hardly be heard over their breathing.

When he stiffened, she glanced back. "What's wrong?"

"I don't have any protection."

"I don't care." She meant it. The promise of ecstasy was too alluring, too tempting. She'd only felt this way once before, and she'd gotten a daughter out of it. Hard to claim it was a bad decision. But even then, the yearning hadn't been nearly as strong. The deep-seated *want* to be with someone with no barriers. To have just him and her and nothing else. So close, there'd be no room for doubt.

"Are you certain?"

"We're both adults. I'm on the pill." The major difference between now and back then.

He rested his forehead on her shoulder, but clung to her. "It's your decision, Kami. I'm here whether I'm inside of you or not."

She needed zero seconds to decide; she wiggled her hips. There were several ways to have fun without penetration, but she was ready for this next step.

He nipped her shoulder. "You're irresistible." A small adjustment and he was pressed against her entrance, his shaft hard and hot.

"Yes."

He entered her. He groaned. "I never thought…" His cock twitched, teasing her with what was to come. Another groan. "I can't believe how different it is. So much better."

She pushed back into him, he went forward until he was fully seated in her heat. He didn't stop, but swayed out and thrust back in.

Her hands were splayed against the windows, her back curved to open herself to him. His hands dug into her hips, his lips at her neck. The sound of his body slapping into her wet heat filled the cab.

"God, Kami. I'm not going to last long."

"I don't want you to." She wanted to finish with him. It felt right. Both of them bared to each other, finishing together.

He snaked one hand around her front. When his fingers touched her clit, she almost collapsed on top of the controls.

He grunted, his thrusts gaining in force. She chanted his name. His touch was magic. She catapulted over the edge, her orgasm slamming into her. She arched her back as she cried out, her voice loud in the small space.

He called her name and jerked behind her. She swore he hit his head on the roof of the cab, but she didn't bother to check, too lost in her own pleasure.

A few more pumps, and they both fell still. He was still wrapped around her, not moving.

"We need to do this more often," she gasped.

"Absolutely," he agreed. "We can have combine sex next month."

She giggled. "We might need to. It might be the only time I see you."

He adjusted himself enough to kiss her temple. "I'll make time for you."

A warm glow that had nothing to do with sex ignited. He'd make time for her. When he said it like that, it sounded like he promised her everything she ever wanted.

AFTER THEY WERE both on the ground, they adjusted their clothing.

Kami brushed her hair off her face. Their exertion in the

cramped cab and the heat flowing into the barn was making her sticky.

Travis finished tucking his shirt back in. He grinned at her. "I never liked living in the country more than I do now."

"It certainly makes spontaneous sex easier when you don't have to worry about anyone walking in on you."

"My cousins might, but since most of them are getting married, I think they'll know what's going on quicker." He shrugged. "But I can't promise they won't shout encouragement."

She laughed and stepped into his embrace. He wrapped an arm around her and they started for the door.

A sharp sound echoed into the barn. Was that a car door? He didn't pause, more used to people coming and going than she was.

"I should've shut my truck off so we could've heard someone driving up. Sounds like we almost had coitus interruptus."

Two weeks ago, she would've panicked at the idea, worried about what people would've thought of her. But not today. She was proud to be Travis's plus one.

They exited the barn. The early evening sun still bright, she squinted at the unfamiliar car parked by the house.

Travis stalled.

"Who is— Are you okay?"

His face had gone ashen, his eyes full of dismay.

"Yeah," he drew out.

A man and a woman were walking up the path to Travis's front door. An older couple, but not any of his aunts or uncles. Good thing they were both dressed and put back together. His hat had never even come off. Her hair was mussed and her cheeks were probably flushed, but no one would look at them and guess what they'd just done.

He gently extracted his arm from around her shoulders

and stepped away. "Do you mind shutting off the truck? It's okay to leave it parked there."

"Who are they?" she asked, but he was already striding away from her. Okay.

Shut off the truck and bring the keys back. She could always park it in its typical spot. The overhead door was still open in the large garage off the side of his house.

"Do you want me to park it for you?" she called.

He turned his head to call, "Sure." That was all she got.

Who was the couple? And why'd he seem so tense?

She jumped in, fiddled around with the lever, and scooted the seat forward. Throwing it into gear, she ambled the pickup along the gravel loop to the separate garage. Once inside, she killed the engine. Wow, the inside of his ride was *fan-cee.*

When had she ever driven a vehicle this expensive? The old grain truck her dad once owned had been older than him. Driving off the lot, this pickup had to be as expensive as her mom's house. That wasn't a hard challenge.

He kept it nearly immaculate, too. There was no trash on the inside, no dust, which wasn't easy living in the country, and its fresh shower scent was all Travis.

She looked around the garage. It was neat and orderly. Like most farmer's garages, there were piles of equipment in corners and along the walls, but there was clearly a system of storage.

How could two people who were raised basically next door to each other grow up so differently?

And how long would it take before she ever reached the level of efficiency of just one of his out buildings?

She steeled herself. No. She could do it. Time, patience, and a ton of sweat equity. And money. Every spare penny she brought in would go to the land. Because her mom and Kambria depended on her. It was the only way to provide a better life for her daughter. So, Kami would dedicate her life to sheep instead of teaching children skills that would strengthen them in any activity, help them build confidence that would translate to any area of their life. It was okay.

Before too many doubts crept in, she climbed out.

Travis and the couple had gone inside. She jogged across the yard, her curiosity spurring her a little faster.

Only the screen door was shut, the main door had been left open. And because Travis took care of everything, the hinges didn't even creak when she entered.

Slipping out of her shoes, she heard low voices.

"Not at all." Travis sounded reassuring. "I was just busy with…ah, work, and I didn't get your message. It's no problem."

Work. She suppressed a grin. Is that what they're calling it these days?

"Della and I don't want to impose," a man replied. "We won't stay long. We figured evening was best and since it's daylight out longer, we don't mind driving home at night."

"Right. No problem." Travis again.

She tiptoed toward the voices. The tension she'd noted in Travis was clear in his voice. Did the couple hear it, too?

They were in the living room. She rounded the corner. The woman looked up in surprise. The man had been about to say something but snapped his mouth shut and glanced at Travis.

Kami did, too. Her heart faltered. Travis's jaw was rigid, and he wasn't glaring at her, but had the look of an over-turned boater without a life vest or paddle.

The woman spoke first. "Did we interrupt something?"

"No," Travis answered quickly. "This is Kami. She's a neighbor, helping out around here."

Her world slowed to a standstill. Those words cleaved the

tenuous trust she'd finally allowed herself to build. *She's a neighbor.*

The trepidation in his body language—he didn't want these people to know he was dating her.

The woman smiled at her, such an endearing expression. "Oh, how sweet of you. We've had such an outpouring of support from our neighbors. Anything we've needed this last year, they've been ready to lend a hand." Her smile wavered, but she cast an endearing look toward Travis. "I don't know what we would've done without Travis, but I suppose we were stealing him away from work around here."

Kami glanced from the couple to Travis.

His eyes were averted, but brimming with stress and sympathy. He finally met her gaze. "These are Michelle's parents."

"I'm very sorry for your loss." Conflicting emotions warred within her. Empathy. Confusion. Hurt. Betrayal. His fiancée had been gone for over a year, but he'd moved on and didn't want them to know. She couldn't understand why he was willing to sacrifice her feelings to spare theirs. No, she understood it, but it didn't resonate with her. They were supposed to be a couple. A pair. Always. Not when it was convenient.

She didn't know his motivations, but she couldn't help the hurt. He acted and spoke as if he was ready for the next phase in life. He'd plowed ahead, damn near barreled his way into her world. When, exactly, should she expect to become the most important person to him? Only when it was convenient?

Was this another situation where he moderated or avoided a topic to preserve feelings, or more like, to preserve his standing in their mind? Paired with his moderation of his parents instead of outright standing up for her and she doubted their future.

How long had he and Michelle dated? Four years? More? Yet, she'd never moved out here and he'd never moved to where she lived. Kami didn't want a future that plodded along because he couldn't commit to his partner.

Kami wanted the same thing, but for her daughter, not for herself. She'd already left her home for someone else, she wasn't going to do it again. When she'd gotten pregnant, she'd had little plans for the future, but she'd had gymnastics and her coaching job. Then Ben proposed and she'd seen a way to improve her future. And she hadn't regretted it. She and Ben had had a good life. But it was over, and she wasn't going to tolerate needing a boyfriend to get others to treat her with respect. She didn't need someone others trusted on her arm to gain confidence.

She laid the keys on the side table with deliberate movements. "If that's all you need." Holding Travis's eye contact, she said, "Then I'm done here."

Spinning on her heel, she squared her shoulders and strode out the door. Travis said something she didn't catch, but she bee-lined for her car.

"Kami." He didn't shout. God forbid he make it look like he gave a shit.

She sped up.

"Kami?"

She whipped open her door and spun on him. "Go back inside, Travis. Pretend that you and I are nothing, and have a good fucking night."

He stopped a few feet away from her, his shoulders hanging like he had no choice. "They're Michelle's parents."

"Yeah, I got that loud and clear. I get that their feelings might be hurt. But what about mine?"

"God, I'm sorry. But I wanted a chance to talk to them first, to ease them into the idea. I'm like a son to them."

She planted her hands on her hips. "I'd get behind that a

little more if I thought you seriously didn't want to make them feel like their daughter's passing was a minor inconvenience. But I think it's more that you don't want them to think less of you."

His face contorted in bewilderment, and she wasn't done.

"The computer games? You like it, but everyone expects you to program or whatever, so you do. You love farming, but everyone expects you to go brainiac it up somewhere, so you do. They expect you to stand by them to try to fill the hole of the daughter they lost, so you do. You were born here and everyone loves the idea of you living here, so you do." She swallowed, dreading her next question. "So if I refused to move out here with you because I want to spend my life on the land I grew up on, then what?"

A muscle jumped in his jaw, pure anguish in his gaze. She'd hit a nerve.

"Then what?" she pressed. "You know, it occurred to me, I've told you all about me and Ben, my hopes and plans for the future, but you've shared nothing. You've given me nothing. Sure, you help out here and there, but you're really not willing to risk anything for me."

"I found Michelle that night. Did you know that?"

She was ready to jump into her car, but she stopped. He'd found his fiancée? How awful.

"I understand it had to be hard."

"It was worse than hard, because I'd…" His jaw clenched, and indecision rippled through his features. "I'd gone there to break up with her."

Kami reared back until her butt thumped the car. She glanced around, trying to gather her thoughts. "And you feel guilty."

"More than guilty. She died by herself, and everyone's treating me like I'm the victim when I was only there to dump her."

"And of course you didn't tell her parents."

"God no."

"They think you're the son they lost, and you don't want to hurt their feelings. You're afraid that they'll think I'm taking you away from them and you're too damn guilty to have an honest talk with them. I'm not your secret."

"Kami." He reached out but dropped his hand, glancing at the house. Afraid they'd see and know they were more than neighbors?

Last straw. "Don't expect any more meals. You and I are done. I can't…I can't settle for being the woman a man has to moderate for. I want to be the woman he'll fight for, the one he'll stand by. Not the one he has to make peace for because no one will accept her as she is. And I'm certainly not going to wait around while you live your little lie so they won't think a little less of you. Because then who do I need stand aside for next? No, thanks."

Sliding into her car, she blinked back tears. They sprouted from anger as much as from heartache.

Careful to keep from speeding, she drove away. No matter what, there were grieving parents in that house. If she'd lost Kambria, a year wouldn't dent her grief. She didn't agree with Travis lying about her, but she wouldn't add one more ounce of stress to the night for them.

She didn't look in her rearview mirror. Part of her was so furious at herself for how blind she'd been to their one-sided relationship. The other part was afraid that he'd be rushing back to the house instead of worrying over her.

CHAPTER 14

Travis lay in bed and stared at the ceiling. It'd been a full week since Kami walked out on him and he'd went back inside and did what she'd furiously recommended. He'd pretended that she was nothing more than a friend to Phil and Della and demolished any self-respect he had.

Kami hadn't called. He hadn't seen her. Their land bordered each other, nothing more. He missed their evening meals together where they discussed their day, the challenges they faced, and just laughed about stupid stuff, like her daily Goldilocks customer—the coffee was always too hot or too cold, never just right.

He'd avoided his family just fine. His parents and siblings were back in their own lives and hadn't so much as called. Texts between his cousins were sufficient. The weekend proved more challenging, but he'd managed to sequester himself in his house each evening after a full day of work. Thankfully, their job could be as solitary as they wanted.

He'd been in bed so long his back ached. Might as well match the rest of him. His head throbbed whenever he recalled blowing Kami off minutes after they'd had sex. His chest tightened when the image of her hurt expression flitted across his mind. The pain in her eyes, the shame staining her cheeks.

Yet he hadn't done a damn thing about it. Was Kami right? Did he feel the need for approval so badly that he was willing to adjust his very thinking, his actions, around it?

No. No one made him enroll in college. It was a basic decision. Leaving home after high school to better oneself wasn't pride. It was what was done in his family. Dad had left the farm for school. Mom had finished her degree before she married Dad. Dillon and Cash left for the army, and Dillon even finished his degree before he returned home. Even Brock had left for two years when his only intention was to come back to work. Aaron…tried.

And the gaming. Last weekend made it clear enough why he turned to his computer for entertainment. A town as small as Moore didn't offer much, especially for a man with no intentions of finding another woman.

Which brought him to today. It was the middle of the week, but he didn't have anything pressing to rush off to do. He'd harbored a wealth of guilt about his determination to break things off with Michelle. Had he clung to it so much that it'd hurt the one he loved?

With a groan, he sat up and stared at his bare feet on the plush carpet, bracing his arms on the edge of the mattress. He was born in this room. This very spot, probably. And here he was. How cool…

Just a couple of weeks ago, it seemed more significant to be here. He got his start here, and it was where he wanted the whole journey to take place.

His land. He squinted outside. Obnoxiously bright and sunny, hardly a cloud in the sky.

His lip curled into a snarl. Why couldn't it fucking rain?

His phone rang.

Who the hell would call at— What time was it?

He blinked at the clock. Whoops. Nine thirty. Almost three hours later than he usually woke.

Glaring at the screen, he snatched it up when he saw it was Justin. "Yeah?"

"Nice to hear from you, too, bro," Justin snapped.

Travis drew his brows down. He'd been a little harsh when he answered, but Justin wasn't usually that sensitive. "I'm waiting for the bad news, because you never call."

"I call all the time."

"You text. Once a month."

A gusty exhale came over line. "Can I stay with you for a while?"

"How long's a while?" Of course, Justin could stay here, but the price was going to be information from his notoriously closed-off brother.

"Until I find a place of my own."

"What? Did you quit your job?"

"You could say that." Travis refused to respond until Justin elaborated. "Fine. I had a disagreement with my boss and I got fired."

"What kind of disagreement?"

"One where I told her to mind her own business," Justin said dryly.

Travis smiled even though it was the last thing he felt like doing. "Point taken. Go ahead and stay here as long as you need to. But if you think my questions are bad, wait until Mom and Dad find out you're moving back to Moore."

"I won't be interrupting anything with you and Kami, will I?"

Ah shit. Now he was in the same boat as Justin. Not wanting anyone up in his personal business. "She and I aren't a thing anymore."

Justin hesitated for a heartbeat. "But you paraded her by

Mom and Dad as if to tell them to get the fuck over it, you run your own life."

Travis groaned. "Not you, too. What is it with everyone thinking my mommy and daddy hold my hand through everything?"

"You're the number one son." Said without heat or venom. A plain statement, like it was a fact Justin truly believed and had accepted.

"What do you mean?" *Please talk. Just this one time, share a little.*

"Look, I get it. You were the calm in Mom's storm; Bridge and I gave her hell. I used to hold it against you, but I've gotten over it. It's just the way it is. You're the good son, the one that lives up to her expectations. I'm the kid that gives her gray hairs."

"One, Brigit gives her way more gray hairs than you. She talks about you all the time, only—" If he continued, would Justin find some emergency calling him away? But he couldn't leave it hanging like that, Justin would fill in the blanks in the worst possible way. "Only I think she feels hurt that you don't talk with her, or tell her what's going on in your life."

Justin let out an exasperated sound. "Because she'd tell me everything I should be doing. 'You know what you could do…'"

Flashbacks bombarded Travis. When he'd told Mom he was fond of designing games. *You know what you could do? You could publish them yourself and I'll tell our housing association. They're mostly retired from the Midwest; you have a built-in audience.* When he'd told Mom he wanted to go to college. *You know what you could do? You could go to Fargo for school. They have an excellent agriculture program.* When he'd told Mom he was glad to be graduating so he could move home. *You know what you should do? Graduate school. You're already there. The professors know you, and when you take over the farm, you'll have first-hand knowledge of emerging practices and research. You need to be progressive to succeed in this business nowadays.*

It'd all made sense. His mom's arguments were comprehensive and solid. And she was always so damn proud when he carried out her dreams.

Hers, not his.

He buried his head in his hands. Kami's accusation was indeed accurate.

But that didn't change the incident with Michelle's parents. That wasn't about pride.

"And…" Justin paused. Travis narrowed his eyes at the floor. A second favor. That had to be killing his brother. "Do you guys have any work for me to do? I have a little financial cushion, but I'd hate to run the well dry."

"Yeah." He winced. Answering before even asking the other four wasn't a good idea. But they were family, and family took care of each other. "Let me talk to the others. But you know we'll help you out."

"Great. I'll be back in a few weeks."

He said his goodbyes to Justin and tossed the phone on his bed. Stretching his arms wide over his head, he inhaled deeply. Then inhaled again. Was that smoke?

He wasn't burning anything. Neither were his cousins. They always arranged burns ahead of time. Letting a burn bin or grass fire get out of control could devastate their operation.

He threw on the nearest clothing he could find and took off out of the room. Then backtracked for his phone in case he had to call the fire department. He stomped into a pair of boots before jogging out the door.

Sniffing the air, he spun around in his yard. Nothing on his property. He needed to get beyond his trees to see if the fields or pastures were in trouble.

He sprinted to his truck and hopped inside. Driving past the trees, he rubbernecked as much as he could.

There. Smoke billowed from—

Shit. Kami's north pasture.

It was the middle of the week. She'd be working. Was there any chance Pam was doing a controlled burn?

Of course not. Pam hadn't done anything with the place, controlled or otherwise, since Earl died.

He palmed his phone as he sped down the road and thumbed through his contacts until he found Deputy Max. They'd grown up with him, and after some vandalism and arson troubles regarding their property, he was programmed into all their phones. Max was old school and didn't mind getting called directly.

When Max answered, Travis didn't hesitate. "Has Pam English notified anyone about a controlled burn?" Giving the rural fire department a heads up wasn't standard, but one could hope.

"Let me check." Max's voice grew muffled as he spoke into his radio. Other voices drifted over the line. Finally, Max came back. "No one's heard anything. What's burning?"

"Something in the north pasture closest to my property, from what I can tell."

"Got it. I'll radio it in."

Travis disconnected and tossed his phone onto his seat. He sped down the gravel road and spun out onto the highway. In less than a minute, he turned onto the road to Kami's. He slowed as he neared the pasture the smoke originated from. Embers glowed throughout blackened grass. The flames weren't high, but the line of fire advanced at a steady pace. A quarter of the pasture had burned.

He found an approach on the other side to park. A place where he'd be out of the way of the rural fire department when they came.

The strong stench clouded the pickup cab. Wind buffeted the smoke in the other direction, but the line of fire spread across the entire pasture, from what he could tell. He got out and walked down the road. Grass smoldered in every direction.

What the hell started this? There'd been no storms. She had no electrical fence that could malfunction. It was possible she'd taken a day off for a controlled burn that got out of hand.

Arson? No. He didn't want to go down that messy road. They'd barely recovered from the last one.

He strode back to his truck. No sirens echoed in the distance yet. The fire department would be there soon, but the rural fire department took a few minutes longer, waiting for their volunteers to arrive.

He coughed as he grabbed his phone, hoping the firemen could put out the fire before it spread to any more of Kami's land, or his family's.

"Yeah," Cash answered.

"Do you see it?"

"*Fuck*. I thought I smelled it. Is that a grass fire?"

"In the English north pasture."

Cash let out a string of swear words. "Well, the cattle will move to the far end, but I'll call Dillon, Aaron, and Brock in case we need to herd them into other pastures to get them away." Cash was gone before the next breath.

Sirens. Finally. Where was Pam? Did she even know her property was burning up?

Billows of dust rose from the engines as they flew down the dirt road. Travis hung back and let them do their thing. The chief took a minute to talk with him, but Travis didn't have any more to tell him.

He brought up Pam's number. She answered with her familiar smoker's growl.

"Are you at home? Your north pasture's on fire."

"Shit. No. I'm at Doc's. Have you called Kami yet?"

His chest tightened. Should he have called her first, or was he avoiding it? No, not with something this important. She was at work, and it was still Pam's property. "No, I'll let you break the news. She might take it better coming from you."

"I thought you two—never mind. None of my business; she'll tell me what she wants. How the hell did the fire start?"

"The firemen are still putting it out. Maybe they'll know something shortly."

They both hung up. Travis's fingers itched to dial Kami's number, but after the way they parted, she didn't need him mucking up the waters.

The fire chief was wading back to him, his smudged yellow firefighting outfit stark against the charred black land behind him.

Travis started toward him, but the chief waved him back. "It's a mess," he called. "The fire didn't originate in this pasture. Do you know if there was anything in the adjacent field?"

Why the field? "No, Kami was concentrating on the pastures to ready them for livestock. She didn't have the equipment to worry about the fields."

The chief's dark brows scrunched together. "Well, they won't be fit to hold anything this year. A year and fresh growth from now, maybe." He squinted into the distance, toward the field he'd asked about. "It's that copse of trees there I'm suspicious of."

Travis followed his gaze. A copse of weathered trees had formed in the middle of a low area of the quarter that was usually too wet for decent planting and definitely too soft to tolerate a tractor's weight. A pile of rocks plucked from the ground over the years was situated next to it. Tendrils of smoke rose from the trees and now that he was looking directly at them and not concentrating on the pasture, it was clear the trees had suffered burn damage.

"How would it start there?" he asked, but his heart was sinking. Experience was already telling him the obvious.

"Stupid kids. Probably have been partying in there for years. The trees can hide a couple of vehicles and it's July, not as wet as the spring months."

"But it's the middle of the week." A weak argument. He'd been a teen once, and while he hadn't been like most teens, his cousins had been.

"They could've been out there having a smoke, who knows. And nothing's written down in a report yet, just my speculation...and experience."

Travis nodded. Chief was likely right. Kids could sniff out any place that smacked of privacy. Most knew the Walkers monitored their property carefully. But English land...

Studying the area, he shook his head. The scent of the grass fire clung to him. He smelled like a joint, which ironically, was what the kids were probably smoking in those trees. His side of the road was clear, green pastures, spattered with wildflowers and fences that had seen better days. In front of him was blackened land surrounded by fencing that'd need to be replaced. New post and wires could replace the old with several hours of back-breaking effort, and the land would recover more fertile than before because of the nutrients left behind.

But his concern was how Kami would recover from the setback.

CHAPTER 15

I can't recover from this. Kami faced the ravaged pasture, tears burning the back of her eyes. She couldn't cry, not in front of her mother.

Mom had withstood Dad's outbursts and crazy decisions, she'd weathered his death, all with a stoic expression and a straight spine. Mom didn't put up with weakness. Kami hated to show any around her.

"The earth will bounce back. It's what it does," Mom said.

But would she? It'd been two days, and the fire department had given them the all clear. No more smoke curled from the ground, and it'd all been drenched so thoroughly an ember would have to possess supernatural powers to grow into a fire.

The old wood fence posts were nothing but nubs. The firemen had busted through one huge section of fencing and the rest hadn't tolerated the heat.

So much for ranching sheep. The funds she'd use to start her ranch would now be diverted to rebuilding fucking fence, down to each and every post. She had two other pastures she could use, but they both bordered this one and shared the string of fence line.

How long would it take to replace—by herself? She'd have Kambria's help some days, and yes, the girl would have to learn how to work on the ranch, but she was still a kid. She could hold wire, fetch tools, and the rest of the time she'd be in her philosophical wonder world of cartwheels, front rolls, and kittens.

And that'd be the extent of her activity. Because replacing all the fencing and purchasing the tools would eat into her allotted funds. So to buy even twenty head of sheep would be a financial burden. Kambria's extracurricular activity would be work and more work, like Kami's. And not even work she was thrilled about.

As she gazed at the destruction, waiting for the surge of "let's do this," the moment when ambition flooded her and she rolled up her sleeves and waded in. It didn't arrive. Why?

Because ranching wasn't in her blood as much as she thought it should be. Just like she wasn't as important to a certain farmer and rancher nearby.

She ground her teeth together. Travis had spotted the fire first, called the fire department and then Mom. He hadn't called her. Was he afraid of how she would've reacted? Or just had gotten what he needed from her?

Her emotions in that regard didn't matter. Because as she looked at the devastation, she knew it'd only be a minor setback for his family. Cash had monitored his cattle and kept them safe. It she'd had any livestock, she'd have been at work and they'd have either succumbed to the fire and smoke, or busted through the gate and gotten miles away before she even untied her apron.

The Walkers would have this fence fixed in a few weeks at the most. Just like they'd hauled the cars out in a few days. They could even have planted a crop in the empty fields.

A hot tear rolled down her cheek.

What had she been thinking? *If you can't do it right, kid, why do it at all?*

Yes, Dad. Why do it at all when she didn't really *want* to? Kambria would be coming home soon, and what if Ben's parents started in on how her daughter was alone too much? What if they—

Kami closed her eyes. She'd never voiced this fear, but it'd always been there, festering. What if they started lobbying for how good the schools were in Normandy? How they could take her to school and pick her up, even afford gymnastics on top of it.

She seethed with anger just anticipating it.

She was not going to give up on Kambria.

But in order to keep the most important thing in her life, she couldn't be selfish. At the same time, she couldn't let fear stop her. She'd abandoned her plans so easily when another option had come by, a "safer" choice.

That choice went up in flames. It was time to face her future.

Trudging back to her old pickup, she stared at her booted feet. Her last weekend alone where she could wallow in all the self-pity she wanted before Kambria came back. Then they could plan school shopping and… Kami gulped. Look for a small house to buy with Ben's life insurance.

She slid inside the pickup and started it. Yep. No matter what, that money was going to the betterment of Kambria's life. That was what Ben had intended.

Driving slowly back home, she let her decisions sink in. They gutted her, but they were right. Maybe if she would've tried last summer, but the life's lessons pressed upon her this summer destroyed her. She had to think with a mother's mind, not a wishful little girl.

Because what if she couldn't parent right?

~

HER MOM GAPED AT HER.

Kami twisted her hands together. They stood at the base of the porch. Mom was just heading into town, probably for Doc's place, as was her usual routine on the weekends.

Kami took a deep breath and plowed forward with her explanation. "I don't think the Walkers will play hardball because of the fire. If they want to drop the price of the property, I'll make up the difference, I promise."

Mom narrowed her eyes on her. "If those boys try to do that, they can take my offer and bury it under the manure pile."

"But you need to sell."

"I don't need to do a damn thing."

Kami's brows lifted. Mom's tone was both adamant and defensive. "Don't you want to sell?"

"Yes. I'm sick of toiling through winter only to drive past well-maintained Walker land and massive fields on my way to this dump. It used to be nice. Back when I had the stamina to care for it and before—" She clamped her mouth shut.

"Before what?" *Don't quit on me.* They didn't share much, and it was like her mom was dangerously close to confiding in her.

Mom glanced away and scrubbed a hand over her face. "Before your father trashed it."

"Why'd you let him?" Why? Why had Dad had so much power over Mom when no one else got to her?

"Because this place was mine before he was around, and it was mine after. I wasn't going to lose one bit of it in a divorce, because you and I both know he would've fought over it just to fight."

Totally. Her parents not getting along wasn't news, but

that Mom had so much bitterness over it was. "Then why'd you marry him?"

"Why'd you marry Ben?"

Kami stared at her. Mom hadn't uttered a single argument against Ben. "I know you think it was because I was pregnant—"

"No," Mom interrupted. "I think being pregnant made you consider the idea, and I think you wanted to prove me wrong. Ultimately, I think you were too scared to do anything else. Lord knows your father never did a thing to build up your confidence."

Ditto, Mother. "I could've handled raising Kambria alone, though Ben would've never let me do it by myself." He probably would've moved to Moore to be close to his kid.

"Could you really? You're thinking like a woman who's been raising a kid on her own for two years now." Mom floated down to perch on the first step. "Not many people knew I was pregnant when I got married."

"Wait—you were?" She knew she was born less than a year later. Had they lied about the date?

"Not with you. I miscarried shortly after we tied the knot." She let out a gusty sigh. "But it was already done. We charged forward, and you came along. By then, Earl had his ideas for what he was going to do, and he did it no matter what I said. I should've listened to everyone."

She hated to ask. Speaking ill of Dad smacked too much of betrayal. "What were they saying?"

Mom snorted, her mouth curling in a wry grin. "That a man as old as he was still living with his parents wasn't going to make a good husband. I ignored them. He helped his parents a great deal. But they were the ones that taught him not to bother with anything if it wasn't done perfectly."

"He was a perfectionist," she agreed.

"He was the sloppiest perfectionist I've ever seen." She

paused a heartbeat, a crease forming between her brows. "That's why I didn't tell you right away that I was selling."

"Because no one could live up to Dad's expectations?"

"No. Because I didn't want to see you stuck out here, losing hope because it's not going the way you envisioned, then have you appear in front of a Justice of the Peace to marry Austin, or someone you didn't really love, who didn't really respect you. I didn't want that for you, and I certainly don't want the tradition to continue with Kambria."

"Mom!" Outrage sifted through her but faded fast. What would she have done those times without Travis's help? If she'd been left on her own, with no money, improper equipment, and unsafe living conditions, a proposal from Austin might've equaled the perfect solution.

"I've been there, Kami. It has nothing to do with being a woman, but everything to do with having a support system, and that's something you and I lack. I couldn't do much for you, but when you came out here asking about me selling, I thought, well, maybe it was all I could do for you. Kambria loves it out here. She would've been the fourth generation. Breaks my heart to think she won't get to play with cats, have horses, or run and jump fences. But none of that helps her grow into a confident young woman who won't hand her future to another out of fear and desperation."

"I loved Ben." Everything Mom said rung true, but she had to get that point across. Ben might've seemed like a last-ditch effort, and maybe he was, but he wasn't a mistake.

"So did I. He was a good kid." Mom's voice shook. "When I saw how he treated you, I couldn't *not* love him. I still worried about you. You seemed frustrated, unsatisfied."

"It was normal couple issues. He made me happy. His family didn't."

Mom rose in one swift move, only wincing a little as her knees fully straightened. "Don't you let them trot all over you. Don't you let them push you around. They aren't your Earl." Kami was caught between shock at her mom's defense and the complete venom over Dad. Mom must've noticed. "He was a bad husband, but he wasn't a terrible father. Don't let my opinion of him taint your good memories. But do know, he didn't help you with his constant capitulation."

"You're okay with me giving up?" Kami asked quietly.

"It's for the right reasons. You wouldn't be taking away from Kambria all the things you want to give her by coming out here." Mom laid a hand on each shoulder. Kami froze. This was almost affection, and it was more than Mom had ever shown. "Don't you dare let anyone tell you that you aren't a good mom. I know these last six weeks were hard for you without her. Yes, it was a great opportunity, but so's the summer with her own damn mom. Don't let them push you. Period."

Kami should've burst into tears at her mother's declaration, but a fierceness as swift as the prairie fire raced through her. She was good enough for her own daughter. Which meant she was good enough for herself. And she wouldn't tolerate anyone thinking she was less than, either. Even if she was single her entire life.

CHAPTER 16

ravis watched Cash and Dillon as they paged through the documents. They stood by the decrepit barn at the English's place—now their place, the first expansion of Walker land in decades. They were breaking from emptying the barn before they tore it down.

"The plans she drew up for a sheep ranch are solid." Why was he bothering? He probably lost them at the word sheep.

Cash's hands were on his hips. "They might be, but we're cattle ranchers, not mutton busters."

"A mutton buster is a kid riding a sheep at the rodeo," Travis said evenly. "This is not a kid's game."

"We didn't say it was." Dillon kept his tone calm, even, like he was trying to prevent an argument from breaking out. "We aren't disregarding her plans. They would've worked for her, but not for us. Cattle is our business, and we have the opportunity to grow. We can expand at least two hundred head, not to mention have enough land to grow our own silage. With Justin working for us..."

Cash nodded. "If Justin sticks around, we can actually

purchase more cattle. Hell, he could build out here and ranch two herds and I wouldn't be so torn between locations."

Travis's first instincts were to argue about all the reasons why Justin shouldn't live out here. That was Kami's dream. Had been her dream.

What was she doing now? He hadn't crossed paths with her in the month they'd had the land. He'd even went out a few times with the guys, hoping to spot her, dreading that she'd be back with Austin. But no luck. He fell short of being labeled a stalker by not going into the restaurant she worked at.

But if he didn't appease his need to lay eyes on her, he might have to conjure a reason to eat out in the middle of the day.

"I don't know if Justin knows what he wants." Hopefully it wasn't to live out here with a bunch of cows.

"If he doesn't, we can hire someone else," Dillon suggested.

Cash and Travis stared at him. The idea of hiring non-family working on the Walker Five was just…weird.

Dillon shrugged. "We're growing, our families are growing, and that's just with spouses. When kids start coming, we aren't going to want to work fourteen-hour days all week."

Travis would. What else was he going to do? Develop his second game. Then a third. A fourth. Rake in the money. Or not. And still be alone. Doing a job he used to love but now felt like monotonous drudgery. Working with his cousins used to be the highlight of this career, but now it highlighted the emptiness.

Maybe that was why he couldn't give up on Kami's woolly dream. "I don't want you to brush off the idea of sheep just because we've only ever done cattle. Look at the numbers. Each sheep would bring in one and a half times what we put into it. We don't get that return on investment from cows. Just like the cattle buffer the bad years in farming, sheep would buffer the bad years of cattle prices. Remember when we bought those black angus for twenty-three hundred dollars a head and the going rate dropped to thirteen fifty? An eight-hundred-dollar loss per cow. I don't think sheep will swing like that."

Dillon eyed him with that concerned gaze of his. The one where he was wondering if he should bring something up, or wait. Travis knew the look and his frustration and irritation grew.

Cash, like usual, didn't hold back. "Are you sure it's because you don't want to brush off Kami? You lost her, and this is how you're trying to hang on."

Travis spun to face him, straining to hold in his outburst. "I don't know. You tell me, you all seem to know." He tapped the screen of the tablet. "Look at the numbers. Worst case scenario, we do it for five years, find out we hate everything to do with sheep, then we can sell and use the funds to expand cattle."

Dillon nodded slowly, his gaze wary and darting to Travis's fists. "We don't want to make business decisions based off you losing Kami. Losing Michelle—"

"I lost Michelle long before that," he snapped, then stepped back. It was one thing to confess to Kami about that night, but another to tell his cousins what happened. What would they think of him?

"What do you mean?" Dillon asked. "You two were engaged."

He opened his mouth to backtrack. Yes, they were. It was grief talking, he'd meant nothing.

Turned out, he didn't care what his cousins thought of him. If they labeled him a heartless asshole, so be it, but his silence had hurt Kami. Michelle was gone. His impending breakup was no more and couldn't hurt her. Her parents were a different story. The rest of his family should know the truth.

"I went to Fargo to break up with her. Only she had passed away by the time I arrived." He'd done it. Now he waited for judgment.

Cash opened his mouth, shut it.

Dillon's expression didn't change, as if he didn't believe what he'd heard. "You were going to break up with her the night she died?"

Travis nodded. He and Michelle had broken up before, but it'd always been her idea and his cousins had helped him pick up the scattered pieces of his heart.

"Why?" Cash asked.

"I know what you're thinking." At least he assumed, based on his history with Michelle. "How long would that have lasted, and would I even have gone through with it. Yes. I'd agonized over it, but only because I knew it was the end. She wasn't moving out here. I wasn't moving there. After the last year of our relationship, I just didn't love her anymore. Not like that."

"Do her parents know?" Cash glanced at him. "No, of course not. You're always so aware of people's feelings, you wouldn't have told them."

"You, too?" Did everyone think he was a people-pleaser? That he let others dictate his actions like he wasn't a grown-ass man? "You're right. I didn't, and it cost me my relationship with Kami because they showed up when she was here and I...I didn't, uh..." God that was hard to admit. When he said it out loud it sounded so much more insulting.

Dillon's eyes flew wide. "You pretended you two were just friends."

Travis clenched his jaw and nodded.

"Dude," Cash breathed.

"Yeah."

"And you still haven't talked to Michelle's parents, have you?" Was that disappointment in Cash's voice?

"Would you? They said they felt like they lost a son. How can I tell them I was planning on dumping their daughter as she was dying?"

"The two aren't related," Dillon said. "She was in her house watching TV and she passed away. It doesn't matter if she thought you two were going to live happily ever after. It's likely she didn't know you were on your way to end the relationship, but come on, man. She'd broken it off twice. She knew something was wrong between the two of you. If you had broken up and she passed away, it wouldn't have been any easier. Maybe it was best the way it happened."

Travis swallowed hard. He and Michelle had been good friends on top of being a couple. They'd missed each other's company, but not enough to give up anything for it. "What about her parents? I can't hurt Kami, but this is more than feelings. Their daughter died."

Cash answered. "Here's my impression. It might break their hearts that you weren't in love with Michelle anymore. You don't have to tell them exactly how that night went. Let them know you two wouldn't have made it to the altar if she had lived, but that doesn't mean you'd be cut out of their life. Will it open a new wound? It might just irritate a healing one."

A year ago, Travis wouldn't have paid attention past Cash's first sentence, but since he'd met Abbi, he was more outspoken and less a peacekeeper. "No, they don't need to know about my intent to breakup. I can still help them, but there's no need for a big talk on how I can't dedicate as much time to their business. There's no point now. Kami's done with me."

Dillon crossed his arms in front of himself. "Doesn't mean you can't still do right by her."

Travis wiped off his brow. The late August sun beat down on him, encouraging the storm of emotions inside. *Do right by Kami.*

Because she was the only one he really wanted to please.

"I'll have to tell them in person." The more he thought about it, the more his decision gave him peace. "I'll leave tonight."

"Leave now," Dillon said. "When you get back, you can let Kami know we found the barrels from her racing days. Ask if she wants them, tell her we're thinking about implementing her sheep plan."

Cash ducked his head. "If lambing isn't as brutal as calving, then I'm on board. As long as Aaron approves, then we should pay her for her outline."

Travis smiled for the first time in weeks. "I'll bug her about every damn piece of equipment until she talks to me."

KAMI PATIENTLY HERDED Kambria out of the jewelry section. "That's not what we're here for."

"Ohmigosh, at gymnastics camp, there's this one girl who had blue hair. Can we get blue dye, Mom? Can we?"

Since Kambria had come home from camp, she'd told at least five gymnastics camp stories. A day.

"I'd rather buy you another shirt instead of hair dye."

"It washes right out, though. I can wash my hair so no teachers complain at school."

I don't give a horse's sweaty ass what the teacher's think about blue hair. "Let's stick to our budget. If we're gonna open our own academy…"

She grinned and Kambria squealed. Her daughter did that every time she brought it up. When Kambria had gotten home, they'd had a long talk. About losing the land, her grandma moving to town, and buying a house.

"I wish you opened a place where I could do gymnastics instead."

So did Kami.

So she did. The sale on the old store she'd been eyeing would be final and the real work would begin, but she'd phoned her old coach—who'd squealed like Kambria—for advice. She now had a mentor.

She'd even told Mom. Spine straight, head high. Her mom had just lifted a brow and gave a curt nod and said, "I knew keeping you in that sport was good for you, could do what your father and I couldn't."

Somehow, Kami got Kambria out of the store and back home without breaking her budget. She was taking less bartending gigs, using the gas money she saved by not driving to her mom's constantly. The two weren't nearly equal, but she'd panic otherwise.

The day job stayed until she needed to dedicate more time to the academy.

Kambria gathered her horde and disappeared into her room. Kami flopped on the couch.

A day of shopping with a pre-teen was so much more intense than she'd realized, but they'd had fun. It was a good day.

Her phone rang. She dug it out of her pocket, her lips pursing at the caller.

"Hi, Martha."

"Listen, Kami, sorry to bother you. You must be working this weekend."

Was her tone more *You should be working*, or *You're so broke I expect you to be working*? Either way, she didn't take the bait.

Martha continued. "I happened to talk to the school superintendent the other day." Kami's heart stuttered. Where was she going with this? "Anyway, I said how worried I was that Kambria seemed to struggle with math and fifth grade is only going to be harder. He said they have excellent fifth grade teachers in Normandy and they'd love to help Kambria." Kami's blood pounded through her ears. "You know, it'd be nothing for her to stay with us while she went to school here. We could take her and pick her up. Instead of sitting at home alone and being scared, she could do her homework. I bet that's all she needs."

Kami fought to keep her voice even. "She's starting school in Moore in two weeks."

"Oh, I know. He assured me it's no problem to transfer after school starts. We'd just have to change her address to here."

That sneaky little— "Kambria's not moving in with you."

"Just for the school year, dear."

Her patronizing tone tickled Kami's last nerve. "Not for this school year, not for any school year."

Martha didn't miss a beat. "Don't you want what's best for her? I know Ben would."

"Don't you think her mother is what's best for her?" Kami held her breath for the answer.

"Well…" Did Martha just pause? Was she for real? "Kambria told us about your newest business endeavor." Said like she flitted from idea to idea. "You're going to be so busy with the gym that we don't want to see Kambria get lost in the shuffle."

More of her temper leaked past the weakening dam. "Lost in the shuffle? Or you're sad to see that you're losing one of your excuses for manipulating her away from me for six weeks?"

"What do you mean by that?"

"Why don't you get horses next?" Kami sat up, but tried to keep her voice down. "She loves riding. Why don't you buy a horse farm and tell her about it and all the riding she could do and get her worked up before even asking me. Because let me tell you, that was a dick move."

Martha gasped. Kami doubted it was from the language, but from her actually speaking out. "If you want to talk about dick moves, Kami, then explain why you're using my son's life insurance on your silly adventures and not our grand-daughter's welfare?"

Oh, no she didn't. "Ben got insurance so he knew we would be taken care of if something happened. Something happened, and guess what? I've been taking care of us. I'm using that money to better our life. Kambria was in on this decision, and before you point out her age, just know that two things were important to us: being together and having something we enjoy doing. She didn't think sitting in a house playing on that damn phone you got her sounded like an ideal future. She thought that living on the farm would be great, but when I decided—me and no one else—that I couldn't tick all our boxes on the farm, I changed plans. And it's a solid plan. And if it falls through? I'm out money I wasn't using to float us anyway."

Martha didn't respond.

"And as for fucking math, she struggles in school like I did. I will decide where she goes to school. Her and I and her teachers here in Moore will decide when she needs extra help. Not you, Martha. Never you, dammit. I'm so tired of worrying what you'll try next, so here's the deal. You be her grandma and quit trying to manipulate our lives, and you can keep seeing her. Don't make her pay for your petty actions. She loves you, but if your relationship turns unhealthy for her, or for me, then I'll have no choice but to limit your visits."

Kami clamped her mouth shut. Oh god. She'd gone there. After Ben died, she'd sworn to herself she'd never restrict the rest of the family, no matter how much of a pain they were. But the toxicity would spill over to Kambria and couldn't be undone. She had to set limits and enforce them.

"I can't believe you'd do such a thing." Martha's voice hitched before she broke into loud sobs.

Those limits Kami was so proud of wavered. Was she a horrible person?

No? She tried to explain. "I know you hated when I moved away from Normandy, but I couldn't raise Kambria there. It's a great town with great people, but I couldn't let her see her mom unhappy and doing nothing with her life. I had options here. It doesn't look like much, but we're getting there."

Martha sniffled. "Kambria had everything she needed here."

"I didn't. It might not matter to you whether I was happy or not. It mattered to your son, and I hoped that would resonate with you. I'm not surprised that it doesn't. Not with the way you all treated me."

"We did no such..." Martha exhaled. "It wasn't personal. I mean, it was, but he really seemed to love you. I accept that."

"He did. He loved you, too. We made it work, but he's gone, and I have to make it work."

They both fell quiet. In the silence was a monumental shift. This was the first real conversation she'd had with Martha. Honest emotions, not pretense.

"I'm not going to quit nagging for more time with her in the summer."

Kami grinned. "I'm sure we can work something out. Why don't you give her a call? We're done shopping for the day."

As soon as she hung up, a text pinged.

Cleaning out the barn. Can u come look at stuff u might want to keep?

Travis? She wanted to jump for joy, but there was no hint of "Hey, I'm sorry, I'll do everything I can to make it right, just come back to me." He hadn't called, just let her go.

That had hurt. Still did.

She texted back. *Ask my mom or throw it all out.*

She sat back. Her optimism that she and Martha were on a new and healthier path bowed out to the tiny spark of hope that his text meant more. The rest of her life was an upward trajectory, but her personal life had come to a grinding halt. And that was just fine. She didn't need a partner. She *wanted* one—totally different. She also wanted amazing sex, and it sucked knowing it existed.

It also sucked knowing someone else could have that with Travis. Steam between the sheets, cuddling and talking well into the night. Laughter over food and work stories. Him sharing that with a new woman.

She closed her eyes against the pain. *Hold my limits.*

Her phone pinged. She expected an *okay, thanks* but there was more. *U really should have a look first.*

She pondered her phone. Finally, she punched in, *Why?*

We'd throw. U might wanna sell.

He hooked her with the money. She wasn't a charity case, but if the Walkers were going to throw it away, well…

"Kambria, we gotta run an errand."

CHAPTER 17

*T*ravis's stomach threatened to claw its way out of his throat. He paced the yard of what used to be Pam English's place. Wind buffeted his shirt and teased the bill of his cap. If it got any stronger, it'd blow it off.

Kami was almost here. He hadn't been as nervous as his first and only date with her all those years ago. So much more rode on how this meeting played out.

Would she be open to talking about more than her dad's old junk?

He heard the car before he saw it. Pam had sold the truck. Travis had almost bought it because it was Kami's truck. But it wasn't, and he was already acting desperate enough losing sleep over her and thinking about her all day.

Kambria waved from the backseat. He tossed her a wave in return. Now he knew why all the older people made comments like "I knew you when you were this big." Kambria had to have grown two inches since he'd last seen her. She might even grow taller than her mom soon.

"Hey, Travis." She rushed out of the car as soon as it

stopped and went running around the grassy area. As he expected, she cartwheeled her way there, only his brows rose at her increase in skill.

Kami exited the car slowly. The wind caught her hair and whipped it around her face.

He tried to play it as cool as he could. "That must've been some camp. I can even tell how much better she's gotten."

Her features brightened, but she didn't quite smile. "Yeah. It was."

"Must be good to have her home."

"Yes."

Neither of them were particularly loquacious. Travis adjusted his hat and held in his sigh. His first fantasy was demolished. She wasn't jumping back into his arms. He'd been an asshole and had to prove himself.

"So we cleaned out the barn. We're going to tear it down."

"Okay. What'd you find?"

He let an easy grin spread across his face. "Three barrels, for starters."

She blinked and peered toward the barn. "Really? I'm not surprised Dad kept them, but you can get rid of them. They weren't good enough to sell back then, I doubt they're worth anything now."

There was zero interest in her voice. Her dad had really destroyed her interest in barrel racing, or she hadn't cared for it in the first place.

"We can donate them to the 4-H club or something."

She nodded. "That'd be good. Was that it?"

He studied her. Her shoulders were rigid and she was half turned to leave. He wanted her to stay forever, but she was the one on land that she'd fought to keep and lost. She was the one faced with a man who refused to acknowledge what was between them.

"Actually, what I really wanted you to see is behind the barn. It was easier to place items there once we wrestled the backdoor open."

"I'm surprised the whole structure didn't fall on your heads."

Could he hope that she was worried about him? It was a start, but worrying her wasn't the feeling he meant to give. "Me, too. It wasn't our favorite chore, but we thought it'd stand long enough to remove everything. There were a few disturbing creaks and groans that made us clear out, but we got the job done."

As if to echo his statement, a couple of pops resonated from the structure. A few more miles an hour and they wouldn't need any equipment to topple it.

"You aren't hiring anyone to tear it down?"

He shook his head. "We have the equipment and space to knock it down. After that it's all cleanup."

Her solemn gaze dropped from his. "What else did you need to show me?"

He beckoned her to follow him and led her around the barn. When they erected a new one, they'd add a corral system so the cattle could winter, but for now, it was a clear space that they'd mowed down. The old corral system had long fallen into disrepair and it was one of the first things they'd ripped out. It'd be easier to clean up debris from the barn once they pushed it down.

He stood by the barn and waited for her to find what he'd saved for her. The barn took the brunt of the gusty conditions, giving them a brief reprieve.

Her gaze landed on a long, homemade beam on a pair of legs that stood only a foot high. "Is that...?"

"An old gymnastics beam. Did your dad make it?"

Her jaw dropped and she crossed over to it, ignoring the

three blue barrels she must've spent hours racing around. "He did. It was after he covered the practice arena in a fit when I didn't place at the county rodeo. I think he felt bad, but I didn't care. I'd rather ride horse for fun and practice my back walk-over for days on this." A laugh escaped. "I can't believe I'd forgotten about it."

"I know it won't work in that new gym you're starting, but it's yours and I couldn't throw it in the burn pile."

Her gaze flew to his and for the first time since she'd arrived, it wasn't guarded. "You've heard about that?"

"Of course. It's big news. I also understand you'll be looking for donors and I want you to know that the Walker Five will help out in any way we can."

"Why?" Incomprehension mixed with suspicion in her eyes.

"When the old one closed down, the whole community felt the loss. We weren't in a position to help then, but we will now. No strings attached."

She squatted by the beam and ran her hand over the smooth surface. "I don't have any business experience, it's a little different from ranching."

"None of us had any experience when we took over the farm."

She squinted up at him; he shifted to block the sun for her. "But you had schooling."

"You'll learn what you need to and more."

She rose. Having her this close again made it easy if he were to reach out and embrace her, tip his head down for a kiss. Longing swept through him. He'd busted the best thing that'd ever happened to him.

"You still have confidence in me?"

"One hundred percent." Could she not see how amazing she was? She'd been dismissed as not intelligent enough and too fast to climb into a guy's back seat her whole life, even after she'd been married and was raising a kid. "Nothing has stopped you. When purchasing your mom's property didn't work out, you didn't settle. You found something that meant even more to you and went for it. We're all rooting for you. Your mom, me and the guys, hell, the whole town wants to see that place succeed. What are you going to call it?"

A smile finally lit her face. "Preston's Gymnastics Academy. I know it's plain, but it was important to me to have Ben's name on it."

"Absolutely."

Her smile died. "I'd better go. Do what you want with the beam. I have no place to store it."

"We'll keep it on the property for you." He inclined his head to the building on the other side of the driveway. "Once we empty that out, we'll have plenty of room." She was turning away, and he didn't know what he did wrong. "I told Michelle's parents," he blurted.

She slowed, but she didn't stop. "I hope they took the news okay. And I certainly hope you didn't rush to them and confess just because you thought it'd win me back. You were clear how it might hurt them."

So he shouldn't have talked to them? Was it mixed signals, or did he truly not understand? He rushed to keep up with her. "Keeping it secret hurt you. And I was mistaken about them. They only want to see me happy. I didn't...uh, I didn't tell them exactly how that night went, but I admitted that I'd planned to break it off."

"Kambria! Time to go," she called. She neared her car and his desperation rose. "It's a too little too late thing, Travis. You're telling me what I want to hear, but that's what you do. My trust is gone."

"I also talked to my parents."

Her gaze turned wary. "Okay?"

"I told them that if I was ever lucky enough to win you back, I expected only the utmost respect from them or they weren't welcome at my home."

Her mouth dropped. Had that gotten through to her? Would it be enough to make her reconsider? He dropped his last card, his last chance at proving he was sincere, both about his feelings for her and that he'd committed to treating her the way she deserved.

"I showed the guys your sheep ranching outline, and we'd like to purchase it from you."

Her eyes flared. "What?"

"Whether you take me back or not, we're not stealing your work."

"Travis, I..." She blinked at him and change came over her. Her expression softened, moisture lined her eyes. He prayed it wasn't because she was preparing herself to break his heart.

"Mom, look. The barn is completely empty." Kambria darted inside.

"Kambria, no!"

Travis took off at a sprint, his boots chewing up gravel. Two concerns fueled his stride. The way the barn had protested all day, Kambria wasn't safe inside, and he had to run fast enough to beat Kami so both of them didn't end up inside.

"Wait out here," he shouted as he tore through the doorway.

A loud shriek bounced off the walls and it took a second for him to realize it wasn't Kambria. Old nails ripped against ancient wood.

He spotted Kambria, frozen by the back door, her face pale as she eyed the roof.

He reached her and slowed, but his eyes played tricks on him. It was like he was still moving fast when he realized the barn was coming down.

~

KAMI HAD JUST CROSSED the threshold when a cloud of dust rose and she lost sight of Travis and Kambria.

Her daughter's scream got lost in the sounds of wrenching wood.

Kami would've screamed, but terror silenced her, clogged her throat. The entire structure tipped. The roof caved as the walls gave in, and it fell in the direction the wind blew.

Exactly where Travis and Kambria had been.

The tide of fear broke.

"Kambria! Travis!"

Initially protected by the doorway, she backpedaled outside. Why did the structure spare her, almost protect her, and fall on top of the ones she loved the most?

When the echoes of groaning and twisting wood died down, she ran out and surveyed the building. It hadn't collapsed in a pile of rubble, but had given up being erect.

"Kambria!" She edged around the side toward the back. The walls bulged, no longer able to bear the weight of the roof. It was like all four walls had heaved the roof off it and partially failed. "Travis!"

"Mom!"

Hope swelled through Kami. She followed her daughter's calls. More debris piled around the barn as she neared the back. The rear wall had given out.

She called for Kambria.

"I'm in the barrels."

The shadow of the barn loomed over her and she squatted to search through the mess. The blue of the barrels stood out in the din of dust. Movement caught her eye.

Kambria was crouched in the space between the three barrels.

Relief poured through her, but she couldn't find Travis. "Where's Travis?"

Kambria's wide eyes searched around her. "He shoved me in here and then all the dust kicked up."

A groan that was all man reached her ears. "I'm here."

"Travis. Oh my god, I thought you both were gone." She spotted him stretched out a few feet from Kambria, partially covered by fallen debris. Her terror hadn't dissipated entirely. Both of them were stuck under a pile of barn that was still unstable. "Were either of you hurt?"

"Not me," Kambria replied. "Just a few scrapes. Travis?"

"I'm good."

Kami tensed. His statement wasn't filled with the easy confidence he usually possessed.

"Kambria," Travis said, "do you think you can pick a path through to your mom and do it without disrupting anything?"

"Don't bump into anything; gotcha." Kambria's determined expression didn't hide her anxiety as she started maneuvering through the hunks of downed wood.

Kami crept as close as she could, grateful to see Kambria's limber form navigate the mess. But what about Travis?

Kambria reached the last of it and launched herself into her arms. Kami hugged her hard and squeezed her eyes closed. She opened them and spun Kambria around to get her far away from the barn. "Go call 9-1-1, and stay by the car, okay?"

Kambria took off, looking over her shoulder toward where Travis was stuck.

When her daughter was out of ear shot, Kami asked, "How bad is it?"

"I don't think I can crawl out." She had to strain to hear him, and he hadn't answered her question.

"Kambria's calling for help. Be honest. How bad?"

"As long as Kambria's out, I'm fine."

The adrenaline coursing through her veins started to dwindle. Her hands trembled, and it wasn't until she sniffled that she realized she was crying. He'd rescued her daughter and risked himself to do it. "Dammit, Travis, quit protecting me. How hurt are you? Be. Honest."

"Want honesty? I love you, Kami. I know you don't trust me, but I'm willing to prove you can. The only person I want to make happy is you. Okay, and Kambria obviously. I want —" He groaned.

"What? What is it?" She leaned left and right to see if she could make out more than his plaid work shirt.

"Nothing, I just tried to move."

Her entire body trembled. "I'm scared, Travis."

"'Bout what?"

She wanted to shout with frustration. He had to be only feet away from her, his voice muffled by debris, and she was helpless. She couldn't even sit because if the barn decided it wanted to be completely on the ground, she had to run. Without Travis. Because she had Kambria to think of.

"You," she said. "I'm scared I'll fall even more in love with you and you'll realize that I'm no good and I fail at everything I do, and, and—you won't want me."

"If I've wanted you since that first bus ride, then I doubt I'll stop. It's you getting away that terrifies me." His words were breathless, like he was fighting a great deal of pain. "I'll live wherever you are. Tell me where to move and I'm there."

She sniffed again. The tears wouldn't stop. "You love your place."

"It's nothing without you."

"Oh god, Travis. I'm so sorry. I should've been more

understanding. You were stuck in a difficult situation and did the best you could." Regret built on top of regret. "You'd already showed me how you felt in front of your entire family. That should've been enough."

"It wasn't, and that's what's important." He grunted. Dammit, had he broken something? Been hit on the head? "I love you. Like, really, really love you."

The words were surreal, and scared her way too much in a situation like this. "I love you, too."

"Know what I've been dreaming about?" He coughed and groaned.

Clenching and unclenching her hands, each minute felt like an hour. She kept Travis talking. "What?"

"Building your dream house here, on this property. You and me and Kambria. Reba and a couple other horses. Maybe a few of our own sheep if I can talk the guys out of a pasture."

It sounded like it could be her dream, too. "You don't have to raise sheep just for me."

"Your plans for sheep were solid and if you want them, we'll get them."

A warm glow burst through the mess inside of her. He really had complete faith in her, and supported her. "What about your house?"

"Justin moved home. He can have it. No, I'm making him buy it. I think he earned more than all of us cousins combined." Travis chuckled and barked a yell. She tiptoed closer. "Don't get close, Kami. I know you're worried. It's nothing a doctor's visit won't fix."

She jerked her head up.

Kambria shouted the same time the sound of sirens became clear. "They're coming, Mom!"

Kami wiggled in her chair. Could the hospitals get more uncomfortable ones?

No, she wouldn't complain. Last time, she didn't have a chance to camp out in a sparsely padded chair. When Ben had crashed, he was gone. This time, she relished the privilege of the bedside vigil.

Had it been less than twenty-four hours since the barn happened? It felt like days, but she wasn't leaving until Travis did.

Two broken ribs, a fractured femur, some internal bleeding, and a head wound that had made her want to vomit. The EMTs said that the bleeding was the most minor of his injuries. They probably would've said anything to get her to back away after the fire department pried the roof off him and dragged him to safety.

He'd been through one surgery and had slept most of the time since. The doctor said he'd need another surgery on his leg.

His parents weren't far away, speaking with the doctors. All his cousins had been by to check on him, and most of them were probably still here, filling up the waiting room.

Travis sighed and winced. She scooted her chair closer, but that proved impossible. One more inch and she'd be on the bed.

He blinked his eyes open and smacked his mouth with a grimace. She was ready with the pink foam sponge on a stick. Dabbing off the excess water, she swabbed his mouth.

He let her without protest. "The mint flavor always surprises me."

"It takes the sting out of not being allowed anything to drink." Wrapping her hands around one of his, minding the IV, she smiled. He looked dazed and disgruntled. "I can't believe you were able to have a full conversation while you were in that much pain."

He shrugged, then scowled. With his ribs, any movement must hurt. "I'm not missing any more time with you." His tired blue eyes pinned her. "I'm going to ask you to marry me someday, fair warning."

Her smile turned into a grin. They were having this conversation in a hospital and it seemed completely appropriate. "Fair warning, I might accept."

One year later...

"I guess we should name him."

Travis glanced up from the tiny face he'd been staring at for an hour. His son. "You need to be resting."

"I'm fine. And unlike when you told me that, I really am fine. Trust me. I've done this before."

Kambria perked up. "With me, right?"

"Yes, you."

His whole world was in this small hospital room. His wife and daughter. They were discussing official adoption, and he assured Kambria that keeping her last name would not be insulting in the slightest.

How much had happened since he'd been in this place? He still walked with a limp, but his ribs were healed and he only had a tiny scar on his forehead. Pretty good for half a barn falling on him. Their new house was finished a few weeks ago, in the same place as the house Kami had grown up in. His cousins made sure they were moved in and everything was painted to order, while Kami didn't let something like being nine months pregnant slow down her coaching and running the gym. The projected growth for the next year was astounding, and he promised to strap on that baby-wearing thingy while she studied for class. She was starting slow, but working toward a business degree.

"I guess a name might be in order," he drawled. "When Elle and Abbi have their kids, we can't still be shouting 'hey, you' at family get-togethers."

Kami chuckled. "I've still got money on Abbi dropping first, but I guess we'll have to wait a few months to find out."

"You know my vote for names," Kambria said.

Kami rolled her gaze toward where Kambia was buried in her phone. "We're not naming him after anyone in a boy band." She looked back to him, her gaze dropping to their sleeping son. "Do we go the family route?"

They'd thrown names around for months, had kept the gender a surprise. But really, there was only one name Travis had decided on if it was a boy. He was mostly sure Kami would agree.

"I think Benjamin Preston Walker would work."

Kami's eyes widened. Kambria's head popped up. Neither of them said anything.

Moisture glittered in Kami's eyes. She blinked. Her nose twitched. She waved her non-IV hand in front of her face. "These hormones. I mean... Why?"

"It honors Kambria's dad and a man who was important to you, treated you right when so many others didn't."

Tears rolled down her face and he had to admit to the backs of his eyes burning. Damn hormones.

A tiny squeal escaped Kambria. "I love it, Mom. Do you?"

"I think it's perfect, I really do. But, really? You're okay with that?"

"It'd make me proud, just like you two do."

"OMG. Just wait until I tell Grandma Martha." Kambria palmed her phone and dialed.

Kami lifted her brow at Travis. "I really don't know how Martha will take it."

He would wave her worries off, but his hands were full. "She likes me. She won't take it as an insult. And who cares?"

A grin lit Kami's face. The fatigue of childbirth did nothing to diminish her radiance. "You've been saying that a lot. It's sexy."

He settled back with the warm bundle and one thought: Couldn't wait to get his family home.

Kambria hung up. "Ohmigosh, you guys. Grandma loves it. She said it'd be cool if I ever had a son, he could be named after his grandpa and his uncle."

Travis laughed; little Ben squirmed. Kami's eyes slid shut, and she opened them again.

"Go to sleep. I'll wake you when he's hungry. Besides, Kambria offered her gaming services at beta testing my app and she needs to pay up."

His wife drifted off, his daughter booted his laptop up, and his son slept on his chest.

He ended up with everything he wanted. His home. His farm. His woman. And a whole lot more.

Aaron's looking for love. But he's certain he can't find it in Moore, so he turns to online dating. Will love survive around the world? Find out in Mail Order Farmer.

. . .

FOR ALL THE LATEST NEWS, sneak peeks, and BONUS content sign up for my newsletter.

THANK YOU FOR READING. I'd love to know what you thought. Please consider leaving a review for Guilt Ridden at the retailer the book was purchased from.

~Marie

ABOUT THE AUTHOR

Marie Johnston writes paranormal and contemporary romance. Before she was a writer, she was a microbiologist. Depending on the situation, she can be oddly unconcerned about germs or weirdly phobic. She's also a licensed medical technician and has worked as a public health microbiologist and as a lab tech in hospital and clinic labs. Marie's been a volunteer EMT, a college instructor, a security guard, a phlebotomist, a hotel clerk, and a coffee pourer in a bingo hall. All fodder for a writer!! She has four kids, an old cat, and a puppy that's bigger than half her kids.

mariejohnstonwriter.com
Facebook
Twitter @mjohnstonwriter